*S*ir Ranulf caught the warmth of Isabella's smile and acknowledged it gratefully with his eyes. Fleeting though it was, to Isabella the look which passed between them signified much more than just his astonishing success with her father. It also confirmed, with a painful certainty and clarity, that her feelings for this man were stronger than she had experienced before.

Until that moment she had been able to tell herself that she was refining too much upon a natural fascination with their enigmatic neighbor. Now she knew better, and the knowledge gave her pain because, as her father had just reminded her, the de Hyvilles were only mushrooms, in a different world from the Thrinby family . . ..

Also by Audrey Blanshard:

THE LYDEARD BEAUTY   50016 $1.75

A VIRGINIAN VENNCOMBE   23420 $1.50

Sir Ranulf and the Runaway

Audrey Blanshard

FAWCETT COVENTRY • NEW YORK

SIR RANULF AND THE RUNAWAY

THIS BOOK CONTAINS THE COMPLETE TEXT OF
THE ORIGINAL HARDCOVER EDITION.

Published by Fawcett Coventry Books, a unit of CBS
Publications, the Consumer Publishing Division of CBS
Inc., by arrangement with Robert Hale Limited.

ISBN: 0-449-50081-0

Printed in the United States of America

First Fawcett Coventry printing: August 1980

10 9 8 7 6 5 4 3 2 1

One

The two sisters stepped into the brightness of July morning sunlight, the delicate pastel hues of their high-waisted muslin dresses suddenly thrown into brilliant contrast with the gloomy, creeper-clad pile behind them. They paused before venturing further into the glare and unfurled their parasols; for, although a greater part of the Priory's rugged acres was clothed in trees artistically disposed in groves, clumps and belts, and a thousand varied bushes crept around and overhung almost every walk and rocky glade in the park, the ladies, after a lifetime's experience, knew well how to avoid the more oppressive paths and stay in the warming rays of the sun.

The Priory, with its castellations, turrets and towers, and the picturesque tree-clad grounds, gave every impression of being an antique ancestral estate; but this was not so, anymore than its owner, Sir John de Hyville, was of ancient aristocratic lineage. Only twenty-five years before the Priory had been a modest, comfortable and unassuming house of simple design, and Sir John had been plain Mr Jack Huggins, a mere cit—but far from unassuming.

His father, the architect of his own fortune in brewing, had—as Sir John was fond of saying—lived just long enough to fill his pipe and then left him to enjoy it. Jack Huggins, although only eighteen summers when he came into his considerable inheritance, did not squander it at the gaming tables as his aristocratic counterparts so often did, but became a shrewd and careful investor.

As he chose his acquaintance, even at that tender age, as shrewdly as his investments, and a year or two later had set up house in very good style in Portland Place, by the time he was casting about for a wife several noble mamas had him in their eye for their high-bred but inadequately portioned daughters. Thus he was able to select a partner from a varied collection of ladies of rank, some with a claim to beauty if not fortune; so it was all the more surprising that his choice should have fallen upon Lady Malvina, daughter of the dissipated and ruined Earl Bentwitchen. At five-and-twenty she was two years his senior, and her dearest friend could not have called her well-favoured; her broad features were irregular, and even when she smiled—which she did frequently for she was a good-natured girl—it was only to reveal crooked, if white teeth. Her ladyship was above average height and generously built, but young Mr Huggins was a handsome, well-made sort of fellow taller than she, and she was well-satisfied with her lot—if not her name—when she moved into Portland Place to begin life as Lady Malvina Huggins.

Within a year of his marriage Jack Huggins had acquired a son, a baronetcy, another fortune, a country estate and a taste for Gothic novels. The latter obsession, for such it became, soon had a marked effect upon all his other acquisitions; even the infant John was to be provided with a cradle of cathedral-like proportions and design.

When Mr Huggins heard he had inherited the title from a hitherto unknown kinsman, he straightway travelled north into Yorkshire to inspect the property which accompanied it, although Lady Malvina was not yet out of the straw. But he was sadly disappointed: the Priory was no old ivy-covered picturesque building with crumbling cloisters, but a four-square sensible house in which the bricks had scarcely had time to weather. However, his romantic eye, nourished on the recently published *Mysteries of Udolpho* and alert for such details, soon discerned that the rugged and hilly surroundings held distinct Gothic possibilities, and by the time he returned to Portland Place his head was full of schemes for the improvement of the Priory, so that it should live up to its name.

He too was determined to live up to his newly-acquired title, for, as he pointed out to his increasingly bewildered wife, "Who ever heard of a Sir Jack *Huggins*? I am persuaded you yourself, my dear, would prefer something with a more distinguished and ancient ring to it. So," he went on, drawing himself up proudly to his full impressive height, "I have fixed upon *de Hyville*—Sir John de Hyville of the Priory. Does that sound well?" he asked rhetorically.

In no time at all Lady Malvina found herself encoached with her baby son, who had been snatched from his still very commonplace cradle, and on the road to her new northern home. The Priory was even

7

then swarming with builders, craftsmen and gardeners, and had remained so ever since.

So, twenty-four years later, when two of her ladyship's daughters, Isabella and Bianca, promenaded about the sunny Priory gardens the only unchanged and recognizable feature was the army of men still toiling in its environs.

"You must own it is good to be home again," Isabella addressed her junior, and taking a deep and enthusiastic breath of the Yorkshire air. "London is so dirty and oppressive, especially in the summer months."

Bianca pouted, although this could not wholly mar the charm of her delicate features set in a heart-shaped face, and encircled by dusky curls. It was a mystery to all how the far from comely Lady Malvina had produced such an attractive daughter, although Isabella inclined to a plainness of feature after her mother's style. "I suppose so," she conceded. "And I certainly thought some aspects of Town life to be quite beastly and squalid. All those poor ragged beggars we saw thronging the streets! I cannot believe that only last year they fought so bravely at Waterloo—and to be now *starving*. The perfectly dreadful injuries some of them had I still can't bear to contemplate . . ." Her elder sister was about to advise her not to dwell upon such matters but Bianca's boundless compassion was fully roused now. "And do you remember that wretched climbing boy being dragged along and beaten by his master, as we drove past in the carriage? I shall never forget the look of mute appeal in his terrified eyes. We should have stopped—it was *awful*!" She turned her own long-lashed eyes to her sister, who noted with disquiet the tears that were already gathering there.

"Love, it serves no purpose to torment yourself with these things," Isabella said gently. "There is a good deal of misery in this world, and where one can one must do all in one's power to alleviate it, but you cannot hold yourself responsible for every injustice in London. Nonetheless," she went on in a different tone and anxious to turn the subject, "I collect you were not completely miserable there?"

"Oh no," agreed Bianca readily enough. "How could I be? We made such delightful friends—Jane and Margaret, the Westons, Henrietta—oh, and the Amershams, of course."

Isabella noted the seemingly casual addition of the Amershams, and smiled to herself; Bianca, it was only too plain to see, was nursing a violent *tendre* for young Carleton Amersham. But she forebore to tease her: it had been Bianca's first season and she had conducted herself in the most exemplary fashion; her head had not been turned in the smallest degree by a host of admirers, and her behaviour, for one of only seventeen, had been amazingly dignified. Isabella thought back over three years to her own come-out and doubted her conduct had been as praiseworthy. Also, for the latter days of their stay in London, the steadying influence of their mama had been absent. But John, their elder brother, had been with them and was now left behind in Town: he was determined to witness the opening of the new Vauxhall Bridge.

The ladies were now approaching a half-ruined Gothic dairy, which had never seen a dairymaid or a churn of milk, and which was one of the many build-

9

ings scattered about the Park over the years by Sir John.

"It was a great shame," Isabella remarked, "that mama was called away so precipitately—otherwise I daresay she might have invited the Amershams to the Priory. You must know they reside not very far distant—in the West Riding, I believe Julia said."

"Oh yes," Bianca returned with wonderful indifference but a revealing blush. "I did hear something of the sort. How do you think Hippolita goes on?" she asked, reverting to their mother's absence: Lady Malvina had been summoned ten days before to her eldest daughter's imminent lying-in at her home, Flaxby House near Harrogate.

"Don't fret about Polly. I am persuaded she will do very well—she was blooming according to last reports."

"But shouldn't it all be over by now?" Bianca asked. "I do hope mama is not keeping bad news from us."

"I am sure that is most unlikely," Isabella sought to reassure her, but was interrupted by an even more pressing and immediate anxiety.

"Oh, the *poor* little bird!" cried Bianca. "Look, there, beneath the lilac!"

Isabella followed her gaze with some apprehension as she faced the prospect of another harrowing scene with her tender-hearted sister. "No, don't approach it too closely—you will frighten it half to death," she warned. "I fear it has broken its wing."

"Oh *no*! I cannot bear to look . . ."

"No, love, I should not," recommended Isabella as she saw the inevitable tears welling up in her eyes.

10

"Walk on to the summer-house and I will come to you there."

Bianca threw her a horror-stricken glance. "What are you going to do?"

"It must be put out of its misery—it is the kindest way."

"You're not—? You couldn't—?"

"No, of course I shan't do it myself. Now, please, do you continue your walk."

Isabella soon discovered one of their ubiquitous gardeners, busy with a hoe, and asked him to despatch the bird: she waited until she was satisfied he had done her bidding, and then hastened to the summer-house.

"There, it is all over," she told Bianca, who was sitting inside the musty stone building. Her face was concealed beneath the poke of her French bonnet but she appeared to be studying with fixed gaze the parasol resting upon her lap.

"I don't know how you can do such things," she said in a small voice.

"If you think about it you will surely agree it would be a good deal worse to have left it for a cat to find," Isabella remarked bluntly, well used to scenes of this nature; for although an excess of sensibility might have been endearing when Bianca was a child, it was fast becoming an embarrassment now.

Bianca sighed and rose to her feet. "Yes, I expect you are right . . ."

"Come, let us continue our stroll," Isabella said encouragingly, hoping that no more harrowing sights would assail their eyes. However, before she left the subject, she took the opportunity to offer some sisterly advice. "Do endeavour to curb your display of lacerated sentiments a trifle, love, otherwise you may make everyone about you feel perfect heartless beasts—and that is really not so. But when you do encounter others' misfortunes, just pause to ask yourself, Is there anything I can do to relieve their suffering? If there is, then help them with as little ado as possible: if not, try to accept it without too much distress." She gave a deprecating little laugh. "I'm sorry! You will be thinking me a veritable Mrs Chapone if I continue in this vein!"

"You make it sound so easy, but I *do* get upset."

"I know you do, and I assure you it is not easy for anyone . . . Goodness, what new freak has got into papa's noddle this time, do you suppose?"

The sisters had reached the spot where the main waterfall tumbled into a deep pool before pursuing a most devious and stony course through the Park. By much artifice and planting of trees and shrubs, the fall, with a cascade of barely twelve feet, had been made to look, over the years, at least twice as impressive. Now a number of men wielding picks were hewing out the stone in the tall bank not far from the water's edge, and causing a great dust and disturbance in one of Isabella's favourite and tranquil corners. Customarily damp, the prolonged hot weather had parched even this ground.

As soon as the ladies were seen approaching, the workmen seized upon the excuse to pause in their exhausting labours, and when the air had cleared a little Sir John was revealed in their midst surveying the operation.

He clambered out over the rubble, beating clouds

of dust from his coat-sleeves, and then removed his tall beaver hat and subjected that to the same brisk treatment. The years had dealt kindly with Sir John: whilst he had been intent upon changing every building and view about him, the only alteration in his own appearance had been the addition of a few wrinkles about his genial blue eyes and a grey streak or two in his dark thatch of hair. Stepping nimbly upon the artful stones in the stream, he came towards his daughters.

"Well, girls, so there you are! And what think ye to my new improvement?—isn't it splendid?"

This was the first sight Isabella and Bianca had had of their parent since returning the previous night after an absence of some months, but they were well-used to his ways and took no affront at this casual greeting. Had there been the slightest thing amiss upon their arrival Sir John would have made it his business to be on hand, but otherwise the Priory and its improvements ranked first with him above all else: it had been so as long as his family could remember.

"Papa, it's good to see you!" Isabella planted a kiss on his brown cheek. "Even if you are as dusty as the gargoyles in the Great Hall!"

"Saucy puss!" he retorted with a cheerful grin, for the many years of surrounding himself with Gothic gloom and melancholy had left his naturally buoyant nature quite unscathed. He turned to his youngest daughter and pinched her chin, as if she were still seven years old and not a dignified seventeen.

Bianca did her best to conceal what she knew to be unreasonable annoyance at this parental gesture, but

13

she could not refrain from declaring: "*Splendid*, you say, papa? I think it's a perfectly horrid hole and no more."

He surveyed his unappreciative offspring under raised brows. "Do you, indeed? That, I would have you know, my dear Bianca, is a hermit's cave," he told her proudly.

Isabella bit her lip to suppress the smile that rose unbidden, and fixed her gaze upon the reflection of the gaping hole in the pool.

But Bianca, as always, was hot on the heels of any suspicion of heartlessness. "You do not mean to *incarcerate* some poor wretch in there, do you, papa?" she asked in shocked accents.

"Well, puss, I had thought that One-eyed Jack from the village might welcome the offer of such picturesque shelter, you know."

Isabella stole a sideways glance at him to determine if he were serious or not in this intention, but it was impossible to discern anything from those twinkling blue eyes. She considered it wise to divert her sister's attention from the future fate of One-eyed Jack. "How deep do you propose to make the cave, papa?"

This enquiry had the desired effect: any question of an occupant was entirely forgotten in discussion of the difficulties of the construction, and the absorbing interest of the final embellishment of such an unusual dwelling.

"It will be beastly dark in there—and damp," said an unimpressed Bianca with a shudder: she feared her father had ignored how wet their climate customarily was.

14

"But it is to be lined with tropical shells of surpassing beauty and iridescence," protested Sir John, never one to be unduly concerned over practicalities; or perhaps, thought Isabella, he expected them to impart some latent heat from their native torrid clime. "I travelled to Liverpool myself to select the prime specimens, as soon as I had word the ship from the South Seas had docked. They are this moment housed in the pinery—you must see them."

This caused Isabella to reflect further that this circumstance made the shells the only things of a tropical nature ever to inhabit the pinery, for pineapples had certainly never flourished therein: but she forebore to say so. Instead, she told her father they would, of course, look in there on their way back to the house, but that for the moment they would walk to the belvedere. The latter was situated almost on the boundary of the Park, where the de Hyville land marched with that of neighbouring Thrinby Hall.

The belvedere, an immensely tall triangular structure with three turrets, Sir John reckoned to be one of his most impressive achievements, exceeded only by the refashioning of the Priory itself, and usually he could be depended upon to bridle up at its very mention. So Isabella was surprised to see that her remark had now brought a frown to his brow. "Take care when you approach the boundary," he told them. "Young Thrinby is soon to return, I hear."

Bianca looked suitably awed by this intelligence, but Isabella gave a peal of laughter. "Papa, I cannot conceive why you persist in your belief that Sir Ranulf is an ogre, or worse, when everyone else maintains—"

"Never mind that," he said in unwontedly terse accents. "I want no truck with Thrinbys, old or young, and there's an end to it."

When the sisters were out of earshot of their parent, Bianca reverted to the vexed question of the Thrinby family. "Why does papa so dislike our neighbours, do you know? If Sir Ranulf is really so threatening, perhaps we shouldn't encroach upon his boundaries at all."

"Don't be such a gudgeon!" Isabella exclaimed. "There is a six-foot wall between us, you know, and in any event the most tyrannical and irascible gentleman could scarcely object to us walking in our own park! I fancy papa's dislike probably has its roots in some trivial squabble years ago," she went on in an attempt to depress her sister's irrational fears. "Gentlemen can fall out over the stupidest things at times. Besides, I am not sure he has even met the present Sir Ranulf, who is from home a great deal, I collect. And old Sir Ranulf died only last year, of course. One might have supposed the feud, whatever it was, might have perished with him," she reflected, then added briskly: "But pray don't take it to heart so! Papa is a dear man, and we know he wouldn't harm a fly, but he *is* a trifle eccentric in his ways. There's no denying that could have led to sad misunderstandings with those who do not know him well."

"Do you suppose he will really put One-eyed Jack in that horrid cave?" asked Bianca next; not wholly convinced of even her parent's benevolence, let alone that of the new Sir Ranulf.

"I beg leave to doubt it—but even if he did, I daresay it would be a home of untold luxury compared to

16

the leaky hovel he lives in now," Isabella observed, forgetful of the effect of this disclosure upon her audience.

"Oh! Does he? *Poor man!*" Bianca cried, quite stricken.

Drastic measures were called for, Isabella decided. "I saw Sir Ranulf once," she announced hastily, "and I must say he looked most unlikely to cast the evil eye upon anyone." Although, in fact, he had favoured his young neighbour with a smile which had more than a touch of wickedness in it, and which had thrown her into some confusion. That she should not have mentioned their encounter to her father was understandable, but for some reason she had never revealed it to her sister either until now.

"You did?" exclaimed a wide-eyed and successfully diverted Bianca. "You never told me! What does he look like?"

"Oh, nothing out of the ordinary—dark, about thirty-ish, elegantly dressed—for these wild parts, in any event. Oh, yes," she interposed, "and a most skilful rider, I would hazard. I had Jenny with me, and you know how she *would* bark at horses when she was a puppy? Well, she came very near to unseating Sir Ranulf that day."

"Bella!—what if she had? Think of papa and the kick-up there would have been!"

Isabella had done so, frequently, and even now just to recall the incident disturbed her: it would have been easy, she had thought many times since, to have fancied herself in love with their mysterious neighbour. But being a young lady of good sense she did not allow herself to do so; it would have been no

17

more absurd for her to cry for the moon than dangle after Sir Ranulf.

The belvedere was before them now, casting its great shadow upon them. "Shall we climb to the top of one of the towers?" Isabella suggested. "It is such a beautiful day and we should be able to see for miles."

"Is it still safe?"

"Of course it is! We all know papa intends his buildings to endure for posterity. No flimsy pearwood and plaster structures for him, as you've heard him say a thousand times!" she chuckled, as she opened the studded door and led the way in.

But Bianca had never taken a great interest in her papa's obsession, and was now more concerned with avoiding the spiders' webs inside the belvedere. After uttering a few peevish complaints, which rang in a hollow fashion about the spiral stairs, she reserved her breath for the long climb.

When the girls debouched into the open air again and walked to the parapet wall, the sun was even more blinding than it had been when they set out from the house. They hastily unfurled their parasols.

"We shall be abominably burned in no time!" Bianca objected, puffing out her cheeks in an unladylike fashion. "I am going down again."

"Yes, it is *very* hot," her sister admitted, shading her eyes. "But I must just take a look at the prospect." In truth, it was Thrinby Hall she wanted to see: partly because the house, unlike their own, was genuinely ancient and mysterious-looking; and partly in the hope of catching a glimpse of its owner—if, as papa had said, he was about to return.

But nothing seemed to stir over the heat-hazed

18

vista: the pinnacles and battlements of the mellow stone Hall shimmered, and diamond flashes of sunlight caught the odd pane in the tall leaded windows. The Thrinby estate, a good deal less wooded than the Priory's high-wrought parkland, was quite deserted but for the sheep barely discernible in the shadows of the occasional enormous oaks dotted about the landscape. Isabella sighed, and turned to follow her sister.

"What was that?" Bianca whispered, as she checked, round-eyed, at the top of the stairs.

Isabella, too, had been arrested by the shrill screams that shattered the dream-like afternoon and gave it instead a nightmarish quality. "It sounds like a woman," she murmured, but recalling even then the nervous susceptibilities beside her, added quickly: "but it is most likely nothing of the sort—just the Thrinby peacocks, I daresay."

Another distant cry rent the air before Isabella could close the parapet door behind them.

"It *is* a woman, I know it is," Bianca said shakily. Isabella thought so too.

Two

It was not to be supposed that Bianca would forget easily that chilling, horrisonous voice echoing from the Thrinby estate; which, coming on top of the incident of the injured bird, had quite spoiled the sisters' first walk in the park since their return from London.

"Who lives at the Hall now?" Bianca asked, as they walked with perceptibly quickened pace in spite of the heat back towards the house.

"Only old Lady Thrinby to my knowledge—when her son is away. But I believe she has scarcely left the house since her husband died last year," she elaborated, well aware of what was in Bianca's mind: who could conceivably have screamed like that, and why? "They have maidservants, of course . . ." This time she did not elaborate, being quite baffled by the whole affair. "I will endeavour to discover from Mrs Barnes if they have any visitors at the Hall."

But when approached the de Hyville housekeeper professed complete ignorance of Thrinby affairs. "Sir John doesn't encourage us to go poking our noses into our neighbours' business, as you know, miss," she said, with all the primness of an old servant who knew where *her* duty lay; although Isabella had a strong suspicion that any untoward event occurring the other side of their wall would not take long to be known, first in the stables and then in the servants' hall.

Not surprisingly the sisters had earlier quite forgotten their promise to inspect papa's exotic shells in the pinery, so it was fortunate that, when they all met at dinner, Sir John had received a letter of some importance from his wife. He imparted his news at once.

"I am delighted to tell you, my dears, that Hippolita has a boy."

When he had told them all he knew of the birth, which was not a great deal, as Lady Malvina had rightly supposed her husband would take scant notice of the fascinating trivia connected with such an event, Isabella asked: "Does mama say when she is to return?"

"Not yet awhile, I would hazard," Sir John told her, as he helped himself to beef palates. "If I know aught of your mother she won't rest content until she sees Hippolita on her feet again, and well on the road to recovery."

"But they are both well?" persisted Bianca.

Sir John paused, fork in hand, and surveyed his youngest daughter with a tolerant, half-amused look. "I have said so, have I not? Infant and mother, both, are in high gig. Now, cease your fretting and eat your meat like a good aunt."

The notion of herself in this new role diverted Bianca from her worst fears, but no other topic of conversation was touched upon for the rest of the meal, and even Sir John realized he would command but little attention with his grotto scheme on this occasion. He left them as soon as he was able, saying he wanted to see how work was progressing in the park. In fact, he could not wait to tell Bradbury, his overseer, and the man who had supervised the Priory improvements from the beginning, that he was become a grandfather.

Next day another letter arrived from Lady Malvina, this time directed to her daughters, and conveying a gratifyingly large budget of news from Flaxby House, the home of Hippolita and her husband, Mr Thomas Stokes. Mr Stokes was a Yorkshire gentleman of few pretensions and airs, but with a great goodness of heart which had won the unsophisticated Hippolita's affections; and in addition was possessed of a considerable estate and fortune which had captured her papa's approval.

Isabella applied herself at once to composing an answer to their parent's letter, while Bianca, an indifferent correspondent, promised to add a postscript when she returned from her morning ride.

The day had made an uncertain start, but the sun broke through the clouds as soon as Bianca stepped on the mounting block: taking this as a good omen she determined to ride as far as the lake—an artificial expanse of water created by Sir John solely to reflect an imposing classical folly and picturesque bridge in its depths by day, and the sublimity of the heavens by night. Bianca's reason for going there that morning was more mundane, however: it lay a good distance from the Thrinby estate and she hoped to be undisturbed by whatever unnerving deeds were being

23

enacted there. That they were unsavoury, even horrible, she had no doubt, after her experience the day before; which, she had since decided, must perforce involve some mad female Thrinby incarcerated for life, but lately escaped. (Perhaps the servants were less watchful now that old Sir Ranulf was dead and his son much from home.) Of Lady Thrinby she knew nothing, but concluded it could not be she who was deranged, as some of their neighbours had been well-acquainted with her previously. Of course her ladyship might have lost her reason following her husband's demise, Bianca speculated, drawing all her conclusions from an avid consumption of popular novels. The more horrendous stories, like *The Mysteries of Udolpho*, had been denied her; despite, or rather because of her father's tastes. Lady Malvina had decided that such tales would work so strongly upon her youngest's vivid imagination, in such a spookish house as theirs, that it might wholly overset her reason.

However, it was difficult for even Bianca to remain apprehensive that fine morning, with bird song her only accompaniment, and her resilient young spirits rose as she spurred Dandy into a gallop across a rare open stretch of Priory parkland. Her thoughts turned instead to Mr Carleton Amersham; as they so often did these days. After being advised constantly by her mama whilst in Town to show no particular favour to any one of her several admirers, Bianca now regretted she had apparently succeeded so well in this endeavour. Mr Amersham, for his part, had shown no such impartiality, but had positively danced attendance upon a gorgeous creature with guinea-gold curls

24

and a ravishing smile: the mere thought of Corinna even now was enough to make her gloved hands tighten on the reins. But then, she thought despondently, even if she had the uncommon good fortune to receive an offer from Mr Amersham, she could not see her father approving the match; he was but the fourth son of a seemingly enormous family, and probably had no expectations worthy of the name.

She recalled how he had won her heart for ever while in London, by going to the aid of an urchin crossing-sweeper felled by the wheel of a passing whiskey. The driver of the gig affected total ignorance of the accident and did not stop, although Bianca was sure he must have seen the boy in spite of his excessive speed. The elegant gentleman for whom the sweeper was performing his service at the time, merely raised his glass at the bundle of rags now obstructing his path, and minced distastefully away; but Mr Amersham, then strolling by with Bianca, his sister Julia, and another gentleman of their acquaintance, detached himself from the group the instant he saw what had occurred. In a trice he had summoned a hackney, lifted the limp boy inside, told the jarvey "Berners Street", and consigned the ladies to the care of the bemused and ineffectual Mr Honey, who was left murmuring in a puzzled fashion: *"Berners Street?"* Bianca, who was naturally overwrought by then, had been pleased when Julia answered him with impatience: "The Middlesex Hospital—for accidents, you must know."

From that moment Bianca had been Mr Amersham's slave for life: he had even returned to the hospital a few days later to see how the boy went on, and was able to relieve her anxiety as to his progress. A true Paladin, she thought wistfully; the image of Mr Amersham only fading when she found herself by the lakeside, not a stone's throw from the folly.

Sir John's fancies had taken the form of a Greek temple for this particular edifice, and she rode over to the magnificent pedimented portico to tie up Dandy in the shade. As she did so her eye was caught by a sudden movement between the pillars, and she could have sworn she saw a figure dart off into the shadows. Standing stock still and listening for a good minute, she wondered if she should re-mount and ride on to some other part of the grounds; but hearing nothing besides the ducks' quacking on the lake behind her, and turning to glance at the reassuringly homely flotillas of ducklings—which she had come expressly to feed—she told herself firmly that she was being foolish, and delved into her saddlebag for the scraps cook had given her. She spoke a few soothing words to the gelding, who seemed a trifle restless, but denied his nudging suggestion that he might sample the contents of the packet in her hand.

She walked hesitantly down to the lake but was soon absorbed in the pleasant task of feeding the ducks. It seemed that word of Sir John's dislike of wildfowling must have spread to every duck and widgeon for far and wide, as his lake teemed with them. Bianca did her best to distribute the largesse fairly, and in doing so strayed a quite considerable distance from the folly.

Her peace was suddenly cut up by a blood-chilling yell in the very near vicinity. Dropping the remnants of bread into the water, she wrenched her bonneted head around in time to see Dandy being ridden towards her . . .

She stayed her ground, not from any particular intrepidity, but rather from an instinctive sense that flight would be useless; and in addition she was curious, even in her terror, to discover who the rogue rider of her horse might be. If she could have been said to expect anything at that tense moment, the repeated high-pitched cry prepared her to see a lady riding down upon her; but it soon became clear that it was no female but a small boy, albeit riding side-saddle.

Fright gave way to relief; to be immediately replaced in turn with strong indignation that this strange urchin should *dare* to touch Dandy. As the pair came nearer still she saw that the boy was dirty and hatless: fear rushed back upon her as she thought him to be a gypsy boy, whose family must have invaded their park and even now might be close at hand . . . They were going to steal her horse! —and so brazenly it was scarcely to be believed . . . She looked about her in desperation for one of their gardeners or workmen, but remembered they were all bound to be engaged upon building that stupid grotto . . .

"*Dandy!*" she called out in a scream as the animal swept past her. But her frantic appeal was unnecessary; the boy drew rein in the most accomplished style, and promptly slid the considerable distance to the ground.

"Oh, ma'am—you've given it all to the ducks!" he cried in anguished tones.

"What?" Bianca said blankly, as, in a daze, she

27

took Dandy's reins which were proffered to her by this extraordinary child. She hazarded that he was some seven or eight years old, and on close scrutiny he gave a distinct impression of being the son of a gentleman rather than a gypsy: his skeleton suit had a jacket of red velvet with elaborate frogging and was worn over a frilled shirt, now sadly torn, and with trousers that had probably once been cream.

"The scraps!" he retorted in a voice still high with indignation, and pointing to some very self-satisfied ducks, who were continuing to float near at hand and occasionally cocking beady eyes upon their benefactress. "I *did* so try to reach you in time . . ." There was a pregnant pause. "I'm starving, you see," he concluded pitifully.

Such a moving plea, coupled with a beseeching brown-eyed stare, fit to melt the heart of the steeliest parish officer, could scarcely be expected to leave Bianca's nature unscathed. "Oh, you *poor boy!* I am so *dreadfully sorry* . . . but, who are you?" she asked, caution momentarily overcoming her surge of compassion.

"Don't know," he said, looking away from her and scuffing the turf with his ruined shoes.

"But you must know," she told him forcibly. "Where do you live?"

After a moment's hesitation he jabbed a small thumb vaguely in the direction of Thrinby Hall. "Over there . . . but I'm not going back. You can't make me—nobody could!" he added with mounting fevour.

"But you must—if that *is* where you live," she said doubtfully.

28

He nodded. "Won't go back there, not ever!"

A child at the Hall? He must be lying; yet where else could he have sprung from? "Why won't you return? Are they unkind to you?"

This elicited another eager nod. "Beat me," he declared succinctly. "All the time. Look . . ." He pushed up a rather close-fitting sleeve, and with much grimacing revealed a fearsome-looking contusion.

"*How dreadful!*" Bianca breathed, her eyes round with horror.

"Oh, I've got more of them I can show you," he said, seeming encouraged by this response.

"No, no, there's no need," she told him faintly, as he started to struggle with some of the few remaining buttons on his muddy velvet jacket.

He glowered at her, suspecting her now of only fleeting concern in him. "I'm hungry," he declared, abandoning his disrobing and reverting to his original complaint.

Bianca was beginning to feel somewhat distracted, and wished he would simply go away. "Yes, but I have no food left to give you: besides, you can't live for very long on scraps for the birds."

"Shan't need to," he retorted. "I'm going to join the gypsies," he said all in a rush, and with an excited gleam coming into his eyes. "I saw some in the village yesterday, and they were bound for a fair at—" He paused, cunning superseding his excitement, then added mysteriously: "I know where."

"Oh no! You must not do anything so foolish!" Bianca cried, appalled by this latest disclosure; being kidnapped by a band of gypsies had been one of her chief childhood fears.

" 'S'not foolish—I like horses and they have lots—I could ride all day with them, I 'spect. *They*," he muttered, with a disgruntled jab of his chin in the direction of Thrinby Hall, "won't let me—not ever!"

At this point Bianca recalled the conversation she had had with Isabella only the day before, about helping people in distress. Was this, she wondered, a case in which she should render practical help? Surely it was. A defenceless child, persecuted by his elders—what could be clearer? It was fortunate she had come upon him, and not one of their gardeners who would have been duty bound to return him to the Hall. This decision, however, in no way solved the problem of what to do with him; she wished she knew more about their neighbours. His soulful eyes were still fixed expectantly upon her, and she blurted out: "Look, if I let you ride Dandy part of the way, will you come back to the house with me? I'll ask cook to give you a lovely big dinner," she threw in for extra measure, as she saw his face light up.

He struggled with temptation for a moment, but then said suspiciously: "No, it's just a trick—I'd only be sent back."

Well, he would, of course, and she could see no answer for it.

"I thought you had a kind face, ma'am," he declared tragically, hunching his thin shoulders and sticking his thumbs in the flap of his trousers. "But I see now I'd best be off to catch up with the gypsies." He turned on his heel and started to walk away from her.

Bianca watched him helplessly, completely at a stand. "No, come back, please!"

He turned, readily enough, and favoured her with a long and speculative stare as she hurried towards him.

"Stay! If I promise to fetch you something to eat, will you remain in the folly over there until I return?"

He appeared to consider this offer, then said in a sullen fashion: "You'll tell *them* and they'll come for me."

"No I won't, I promise," she assured him rashly. Isabella would know what to do for the best, and she had to stop him running off somehow. She gave him her sweetest and most encouraging smile. "After all, I don't even know your name, do I? So I cannot tell anyone." She hoped he would not perceive how nominal this reassurance was.

"Oh, all right," he answered in a grudging manner, as if he were rendering her a favour. "But if anyone comes near but you, I'll run, and you'll never see me again," he concluded grandly.

Had his audience not been possessed of such an impressionable nature, it might have been supposed that the latter prospect would be welcome to her above all else; but Bianca took the threat in all seriousness and soon set off at an impassioned gallop for the house. She had such boundless faith in Isabella's good sense being able to extricate her from this bumblebath that she gave no further thought to the difficulties herself, but merely concentrated upon keeping her seat.

Consequently her dismay was very great upon being told by the butler, Staithes, that Miss Isabella had gone visiting and was not expected to return much before dinner. Even that myopic servant noticed the powerful effect his words had upon her.

"Is anything wrong, miss?"

"No—*no*, of course not! I thought I might have accompanied her upon her calls, that is all," she responded, as lightly as she was able, and then made her way across the vast and gloomy Gothic hall to the morning-room, where she had left Isabella writing a letter to their mama.

After a good deal of agitated pacing, she sat down herself at the walnut desk to pen a note to her sister. It was not easy. She knew that whatever she fixed upon was likely to meet with censure, as she rarely seemed to do the right thing in such matters. Suppressing her natural instinct to reveal the entire garbled story, she finally wrote: 'Dearest Bella, Do not fret if I am a little late for dinner. I am acting Good Samaritan to a small persecuted boy from Thrinby Hall. Sorry I cannot disclose more but feel sure you will understand when you hear the whole Yr. affectionate sister, Bianca.'

In truth, she had the haziest notion at this stage quite what her benevolence would entail, but she folded the note and went to place it in her sister's chamber. Then she hurried to the kitchen with a sad tale of Jenny, the spaniel, running off with the earlier scraps, and could she possibly have some more? So *many* dear little ducklings had appeared on the lake in her absence, and she was persuaded they were in imminent danger of starvation if she did not supply sustenance for them at once . . .

Luckily, cook was well used to Bianca's tender-hearted ways, and did not attempt to convince her otherwise; there was one difficulty though. "Bless me, but I've just made a boiled bread pudding, and there's not a crust left . . . There is that pigeon pie from yesterday, but then that don't seem right," she continued doubtfully, but Bianca cut across her.

"That's lovely—just the thing!"

Mrs Woodley's pink features registered considerable surprise on hearing her squeamish young mistress condone what seemed to amount to un-duck-like cannibalism, even in her own robust opinion. Nonetheless she went to the dresser for a cloth to wrap it in.

"—And just a tiny piece of that apple pie too?" Bianca said coaxingly.

"Ah, now look here, miss, they're fresh baked and waiting to go through for dinner," Mrs Woodley protested.

"But there are four pies and only three of us to eat them . . . Besides," she added with a shamefaced grin, "I am a trifle sharp-set myself just now, and they look *so* tempting."

"Well, now, that's different," the flattered cook said indulgently, and proceeded to cut a generous portion. "But don't you go feeding that to no ducks, mind!"

"Oh, indeed no!" Bianca was able to agree in all prim honesty.

Still with no real idea of how she was going to protect the mysterious boy from his unknown persecutors, she nevertheless gathered one or two items together in the small portmanteau—which fortunately was still in her bedchamber from their London visit—and included a comb, a wash-ball and cloth, and a

33

clothes brush to improve the appearance of her young charge. She also put in several guineas, which papa had given her for her stay in Town, and which now she was exceedingly grateful she had had no call to spend. However, she knew how strongly he would disapprove if a single penny of it was spent upon an inmate of Thrinby Hall.

Mercifully, there was little chance of now seeing her father, who, she was tolerably certain, would be fussing over his new grotto; but even so she was greatly relieved to arrive back at the folly without having met anyone on the way there, other than one of their gardeners—and he was some distance away and recognizable only by his blue apron. Dismounting, and taking up the basket of food, she went cautiously between the pillars and into the rather dank interior of the folly.

"Don't be afraid—it is only I," she announced at once to prevent the boy taking flight: but there was no one there. Her eyes quickly scanned the circular room with its massive stone table and carved seats. She set the basket on the table, her young face anxious and frowning. But then, as the minutes passed, she could not deny a sense of relief that she had done her best, but evidently was not called upon to be any more instrumental in the boy's salvation.

"*Yee-ee-ee-ee!*" he yelled, as he swung round a pillar right behind her and bounded to the table.

Her hand flew to her heart. "*Oh . . . I wish* you will not make that dreadful noise!"

"I did that so you'd know who it was!—I'm always doing it."

"I know you are," she said shortly. "I had rather
34

you were made known by your name, like everyone else. I am Bianca de Hyville, and before I open this basket you will tell me your name," she stipulated, feeling that she must know something of this child if she were to help him further.

His greedy eyes darted from her to the basket and back again. "I'm Gordon," he said at last, with the air of one making an enormous concession. "Now, may I have that please?"

Bianca had never heard this odd-sounding name before, and turned a searching look upon him. "Gordon? That must surely be your surname—what, then, is your first name?"

He moved impatiently towards the table. "*Gordon is my name*! Everybody calls me that."

"What is your papa called?"

"Haven't got one."

"Oh," said Bianca, chastened. "—And your mama?"

"Haven't got one of those either," he said dispassionately. "Not any more I haven't."

Now quite crushed, Bianca was uncertain how to proceed after that exchange. She started to unpack the pie. At least there was no doubt as to the fact of his hunger as he munched away, his cheeks bulging out like little rosy apples; although how much she could believe of his other statements, she was still not sure.

"You must have a guardian, then?" she suggested patiently, but that met with another negative headshake. "A governess, or teacher of some sort?" This shot appeared to go home, and he stopped chewing.

"Miss Hibbert," he acknowledged in tones of utter

loathing. "She beats me—they all beat me—and I'm *not going back,*" he reminded her.

So far, then, she had discovered that he was an orphan, probably staying at Thrinby Hall with his governess, and one of his names was Gordon. Whose child he was, and why he was at the Hall, she was clearly not going to find out now that his hunger pangs had been assuaged. Nor could she imagine who 'they' might be, who so ill-treated him: surely not old Lady Thrinby? It could be Sir Ranulf, she supposed; or perhaps he was left wholly to the mercy of the servants? The unpleasant thought then occurred to her that she might have stumbled upon some dark secret of the Thrinbys in the form of this boy. In any event they were not going to be best pleased when they found he had disappeared; but she was quite resolved not to take him back. Thrinby Hall had always been shrouded in a degree of mystery for her, and she was even now not entirely surprised at the boy's story. Nor was she convinced that she had plumbed the depths of the dark deeds that were evidently hidden behind its creeper-clad walls. That scream the day before could well have been Gordon, she supposed, suffering one of his horrid beatings; yes, a safe place must of course be found for him, well away from the village and anyone who might recognize him—and then she would return and tell Isabella the whole. She knew that course could mean her having to face the unknown and angry Lady Thrinby, and even perhaps Sir Ranulf, but she pushed that alarming prospect resolutely to the back of her mind.

"Gordon!" she said firmly, "when you have finished

eating you must tidy yourself, and then we will take a ride on Dandy."

"Not to the Hall," he replied with an equal firmness, viewing her with another onset of suspicion and wiping crumbs from his mouth upon his sleeve.

"No," she promised wearily yet again, and restraining an impulse to scold him for this regrettable habit, "much further away than that—and it will take us a long time. You must behave and do everything just as I say, though, or I will take you back at once."

He grinned with sudden understanding. "We're running away, aren't we? *Yee-ee-ee-ee!*" And, in spite of his substantial ballast of various pies, he jigged energetically around his saviour; who put her hands to her ears and wondered just what she had undertaken.

Three

By the time the Richmond to Harrogate road had been reached, Bianca was prey to the gravest doubts regarding the wisdom of her enterprise.

At first she had been so relieved that they had passed through the village unobserved that little else had mattered, although she had been torn even then between a desire to meet Isabella and pour out her troubles, and a lively dread that if she did so Gordon would be sent home at once. At that point, infected by the boy's high spirits, she had viewed their journey as an adventure: but already it was turning into something of an ordeal.

Fond though Gordon undoubtedly was of riding, he was becoming more and more fidgety, sitting up in front of her on Dandy as each mile slowly passed; and she feared that sooner or later he would tumble off. Also, she was becoming very hot: the now unclouded sun was reaching its zenith, and she was wilting beneath the riding dress of jaconet muslin with a stiflingly high fraise neck-ruff, and thick blue cloth pelisse with caped shoulders. The most sober hat she had been able to find was of black beaver with a single emerald feather, and she could certainly not have worn *that* with a blue pelisse, so her choice had had to fall upon a similar beaver hat, but bearing instead a whole forest of delicate azure plumes. Her intention had been to look as governessy as possible, and she had hastily selected her primmest of clothing; however, she had soon realized that even the most superior governess would scarcely be likely to aspire to such fashionable garments, and she had mentally adjusted her role to that of aunt.

It had also been her intention to ride directly to her destination but it was being borne in upon her that this was not going to be possible either: Gordon's hunger had been assuaged somewhat by Mrs Woodley's pies, but his thirst had not and his constant plaint was for lemonade. Consequently, when she saw an inn quivering in the haze ahead she was not altogether unwilling to halt there—in spite of having little experience of how to go on at such establishments.

The ostler of the Green Dragon came forward, squinting in the sunlight, to help her dismount. The boy had to be dissuaded from following this interesting person into the stables by a promise of quantities of lemonade: Bianca dared not let him out of her sight in case he should disappear. Grasping his recently-washed hand firmly in hers, she ventured through the open door into the inn.

Her eyes took some moments to adjust to the gloom but she was soon aware that several rustic gentlemen quaffing ale were regarding her agape: she tightened her grip on Gordon's hand and was glad, for the first time, of his presence.

40

A rotund figure with bright eyes, and standing scarcely higher than Bianca, hurried forward wiping his hands on a white apron which seemed in danger of engulfing him completely. "Yes, ma'am?" he said uncertainly, almost on tiptoe, endeavouring to look over her shoulder for reassuring signs of an escort or maid.

"We would like some lemonade, please—served in a private parlour," she replied quickly in a firm, clear voice.

"At once, ma'am." He turned away and shouted to the nether regions: "Carrie!" in a broad Yorkshire accent, and with surprising power for one so small.

Determined upon keeping the initiative, Bianca then asked: "Is it possible to hire a carriage—only for a short distance of perhaps a dozen miles, and then back again?"

"Your own has suffered a mishap, like?" he probed cautiously.

"Oh no! I—that is, we are riding, but it is insufferably hot and I should like to continue by carriage."

"Mm," the landlord murmured, rubbing his chin in a thoughtful manner. "This is no posting-house, but we does have a gig for hire—nothing very grand, mind. Leastways we *should* have one, but Mr Jackson took it first thing, and hasn't come back." He was clearly burning with curiosity about this unlikely pair of travellers, and his quick eye went back and forth from the boy's expensive but dishevelled garb to the young lady's fashionable raiment. "I've no lads, though, and you weren't reckoning to drive yourself, ma'am, I daresay?"

"No—yes—that is, I could but—" Her confusion was lost in the sound of a carriage arriving in the yard.

"Mebbe that's him now! Excuse me, ma'am," the landlord said with patent relief, and hurried to the door.

His Carrie, plump and bustling, appeared on the scene as he left it, and Bianca repeated her request for refreshment and a parlour. She was led into another room downstairs, which even on this hot day had an air of mustiness and damp about it. The landlady gave the rough table a surreptitious dust with the corner of her apron.

Bianca had been compelled to drag her charge after her, as his attention was now riveted upon the newly-arrived equipage in the yard, but in the event the parlour window gave him an equal view of that scene. Whilst they awaited their drinks both Bianca and Gordon watched unashamedly as the landlord conversed with a gentleman standing beside a dusty, yellow post-chaise. Well, that wasn't the gig returned, she thought despondently, and wondered what she was going to do now . . . There was nothing for it, Dandy would have to carry them the rest of the way, although exactly how far that was she was unsure, and the prospect of even another mile in the glaring heat was enough to make her weep.

The landlord gesticulated towards the inn and the gentleman glanced across, causing Bianca automatically to duck away from the latticed window although it was highly unlikely that she could be seen. But her apprehension grew with every minute, and even the boy seemed a trifle subdued as he stared at the chaise. Lord, she thought with renewed alarm, looking at his uncovered auburn curls, perhaps he was sickening from the heat of the sun: she should

42

have remembered that he wore no hat. The prospect of arriving at her destination with not only a strange but a sick child, was not to be thought of—and she was really not feeling in very good point herself, she decided with a surge of despair.

Mercifully the lemonade was carried in at that moment by the landlord's wife, and Gordon, at least, revived at the sight of it.

"May I pay you now?" Bianca asked the woman, as she searched in her dainty velvet reticule; she did not want to be compelled to seek out the landlord again.

Carrie's eyes nearly quit their wrinkled sockets as she gazed upon the gleaming gold coin in her palm. "But, miss, 'tis only tuppence . . . Have ye nowt less?" she exclaimed, emotion causing her to lapse into the vernacular.

Quite unused to handling money in the ordinary way, Bianca realized too late that she had committed a stupid blunder in proffering a guinea for a jug of lemonade at such an isolated hostelry.

"Not a three shilling piece—or even a seven shilling one?" the landlady persisted, regarding the gold with awe.

"No, I'm terribly sorry," Bianca murmured unhappily.

"Ay, well, I'll see what can be done, but I'll leave it there for now," the woman said, placing the coin on the table in an almost reverent way.

As soon as they were alone again Gordon's hand shot out before Bianca could re-possess the money. "*Ooh*—a real golden guinea! I've not held one before."

"Well, you have now," observed Bianca in agitation, when he showed no signs of relinquishing it. "Give it back to me . . ."

He put his hands behind his back, then held out clenched fists to her. "Guess which?"

"Gordon, this is *not a game*!"

"Yes it is! Go on—which?"

She set down her reticule and grabbed both of his hands.

"Hey! That's cheating!"

In the ensuing struggle Bianca failed to notice the landlord standing in the doorway in company with the chaise traveller.

"Beg pardon, ma'am, but this gentleman believes he may be able to offer some help, like."

She swung round, her face flushed, and stammered: "Oh! How kind, but I really don't see how he —" Words failed as the wildest thoughts of abduction and robbery flitted through her feverish mind.

"Forgive the intrusion, ma'am," the newcomer said, lowering his head to step into the parlour. "But I would be pleased if you will take my hired chaise in order to complete your journey. I have travelled all day in it, and will be glad to ride the last few miles."

She had a quick impression of a well-dressed, tall man with darkish features; but both of the latter attributes could merely be put down to the fact that they were in a low-ceilinged, ill-lit room; and almost anyone would tower over the stunted landlord.

As she did not return an immediate answer, he continued persuasively: "I have paid off the boys, and they are at your service whenever you wish, ma'am."

It *would* solve her difficulties, without doubt, and suppressing any qualms she had about the propriety

of accepting such an offer from a completely unknown gentleman, she did so with heartfelt thanks.
His slight look of surprise, when he had first seen her,
had not escaped her notice, and she went on a little
breathlessly: "I daresay you must wonder why I am
in this wretched predicament, sir, but, you see, my
nephew here—"(she laid a fond aunt-like hand on his
shoulder) "—absconded from school in the carirer's
cart and arrived home only an hour ago. Luckily, I
discovered him skulking in the garden, and am carrying him back to school with all despatch before his escapade should come to the ears of his father—a fearfully irascible man," she threw in for extra effect, as
she sensed the disbelief in the lazy grey eyes regarding her.

But the stranger merely addressed himself to the
boy, almost indifferently: "Wicked fellow, putting everyone about so."

Bianca held her breath, expecting Gordon to expose them both—and he did say eagerly: "Can we
start now?—I want to see the horses!"—thus betray-
ing an unlikely enthusiasm for his so recently rejected school.

The gentleman, seemingly oblivious of this commendable change of heart, bowed to Bianca. "Well, I
daresay time is of the essence for you both, and so I
will take my leave." He added a cautionary note as he
ducked under the lintel again: "The horses are not
fresh, you understand, although they were changed
only at Ripon. However, I daresay you may be able
to rest them upon arrival."

She assured him that would be done, and thanked
him once more; then the landlord followed him out,

obviously glad to have had this singular problem lifted from his own shoulders with such ease.

"A tankard of your home-brewed," she heard her benefactor order, as she took a hasty sip of lemonade herself before embarking on the next stage of her rash journey.

* * *

"Who was the damsel in distress?" Sir Ranulf inquired of the landlord, as he arranged for his luggage from the chaise to be sent after him. That he had to seek out such intelligence at all betrayed his overwhelming fatigue more plainly than did anything else: and he could almost hear the chaffing comments of his friends; in particular of the now self-exiled Lord Byron, had *he* witnessed his inept handling of such an exceedingly promising situation.

"I'm sorry, sir, but that I couldn't say, seeing as the young lady was a stranger to me—and to these parts, I reckon."

Now Sir Ranulf really cursed himself for being a slouch: the lady had tipped him the double, and serve him right! And as he had lacked the wits to discover for himself even the name of the school concerned, he would not stoop to ask this tapster. He found himself paying for the mysterious maiden's lemonade (she must be wealthy as well as mysterious, if she were in the habit of tendering guineas for trivial purchases) and then put all thought of her from his mind. After all he had only recently fixed upon his choice of bride and it would do no harm, he supposed, to curb his wandering eye just a little—at least until he was no longer an April gentleman.

46

As he rode along, almost lulled to sleep by the potent effect of the heat and the home-brewed, together with the lazy gait of his hired hack, he looked forward with immense relief to at least a month—well, perhaps a fortnight—spent recruiting at his ancestral home. He had just gone through a particularly rigorous London season in this, his thirtieth year, and the weeks of unconscionable late nights had taken their toll.

Before going up to Town it had occurred to him—though not without a certain prompting from his mother—that it was high time he took a wife. So, decisiveness being one of the Thrinby characteristics he possessed in full measure, he had set out with that firm intention, and was now returning home with the mission successfully accomplished.

In the event the task had not presented him with any insuperable difficulties: for he had discovered that provided one did not set one's heart upon capturing one of the favourites in the matrimonial stakes (and in his experience these were, in any year, a bevy of insipid fillies), there was still a tolerable field from which to select one's winner.

The Honourable Helen Rishworth, daughter of the fourth Viscount, although no surpassing beauty like her namesake of former days, was certainly no antidote; and Sir Ranulf considered he had been exceedingly fortunate in his final choice. At five-and-twenty the lady was past the high flights of youth and nor did she seem to be an empty-headed twaddle; by the same token she had seen something of the world in her half-dozen seasons and would not be expecting a doting husband who never strayed from her apron strings. The bluff, widowed Viscount, when approached for the hand of his fourth and only unmarried daughter, had eyed the suitor uncertainly and shown a marked reluctance to bestow his blessing upon the match; but this did not altogether surprise Sir Ranulf. Helen had told him more than once that she acted hostess and generally devoted all her attention to her father, and no doubt Lord Rishworth was unwilling to dispense with her admirable services. The details of the marriage settlement were scarcely touched upon at the interview with the Viscount, but Ranulf was satisfied that his future wife's fortune was more than adequate to enable them to live, with his own substantial income, in a good style.

Once he had seen Lord Rishworth he had no desire to linger another day in Town: the sudden realization of the success of his endeavours seemed to render him acutely aware of his weariness after an enervating season, and his sole wish then was for the peace and quiet of his Yorkshire home . . .

He was now within a mile or two of his native village and, heavy-lidded and hotter still, he regretted the gallant gesture at the inn which had deprived him of his chaise; more particularly as he had bungled the affair badly. But he was too exhausted to repine on that head for long. Instead he cast his mind forward to a pleasant dinner at his mother's table, when he would gratify her with his news; and afterwards would no doubt sleep the clock round with no effort at all.

Sir Ranulf had not sent word to his parent of the exact day of his return, wishing rather to surprise her. In the event, it was he who was surprised—although, in fact, dismay more accurately described the emotion which predominated when he caught a glimpse of the unmistakable mud-coloured travelling carriage belonging to his sister, housed in the coach-house. Such was his dislike of Laetitia and her prosy, tiresome husband, that notwithstanding his utter weariness he was strongly tempted to turn tail and rack up at a posting-house ten miles away. But no: he was damned if he was going to be kept from his own hearth by a mackerel-backed bore like Arthur Beckforth. Besides, he thought, looking on the bright side, perhaps they were near the end of their visit. But if they were not, he knew better than to try to hint them away—they each had a monstrously thick hide, and allusions, however unsubtle, would roll off them like water on a widgeon.

The Beckforths were rarely to be found in their own home, a snug little property in the village of Wimbledon; for although Arthur was a warm man indeed, and one who could have bought a brace of abbeys had the whim so taken him, their preference was for the variety and stimulation of the country residences belonging to their many relatives. There, Arthur found captive audiences for his tedious discourse; and Laetitia, endless opportunities to advise sorely-tried hostesses on how best to manage their households; both secure in the knowledge that as the wealthiest kinsmen without issue in each respective family, they were officially welcome at all times. They held no such powerful attraction for Sir Ranulf, but so long as Lady Thrinby lived it was not to be expected that her only daughter would be barred

the door; and where Laetitia went she made sure
that Arthur followed.

Before facing any of his relations, Sir Ranulf decided that at least he would put off his travel-stained
clothes and dress for dinner in a leisurely fashion. Towards this end he entered the house by a back door
which led him past the servants' quarters. He did not
wish it to be thought he was spying on them and so
he made haste to the stairs which would lead him,
eventually, to his own bedchamber. But the sepulchral quiet which usually hung over the inmates of
Thrinby Hall was all at once quite shattered: a sound
of unmistakable sobbing assailed his ears, and then
two females came around the corner directly in his
path. One, whom he recognized as his housekeeper,
had a maternal arm about the other—a stranger to
him.

It was an awkward moment, and one he could have
avoided only by darting ignominiously into a pantry
or a broom cupboard. Luckily, the two women were
equally anxious to avoid an encounter, and Mrs
Chart, seeing her master was unexpectedly returned,
rolled her already protuberant eyes at him and murmured: "Sir Ranulf, sir!" in a tone of shock; then
bundled her hiccupping charge through the nearest
door. Judging by the clatter and commotion which
ensued, they had chanced upon the butler's pantry,
Sir Ranulf concluded with a boyish grin. He wondered briefly who the devil the distraught female
was, but felt too weary to dwell upon the matter for
long: no doubt all would be made plain in due course.
He plodded heavy-footed up the bare stone stairs.
Gaining the gallery, a cavernous yawn overcame him

just before he reached the sanctuary of his own apartment, and as he sought to stifle it a familiar voice suddenly rang out.

"*Hah! Ranulf!* How like you to arrive just at this moment! You couldn't return yesterday, could you? —oh no!"

He swallowed the yawn and fixed a bleary eye upon his sister, who had unfortunately chosen that moment to emerge from a bedchamber behind him. "No, indeed I could not, Letty—you are in the right of it, as ever," he responded, with a sarcasm which was wholly lost upon her but which at present he was unable to resist. "I had, you see, scarcely reached Tuxford by then. I trust you and Arthur are enjoying your visit?" he went on, making strenuous efforts to be civil. "Have you been with mama long, might I inquire?"

Laetitia was in her early forties, and twelve years lay between her and Ranulf: twelve years in which Lady Thrinby had valiantly sought to provide her lord with an heir—and had suffered instead only a series of miscarriages, stillbirths, and the loss of two girls who did not survive infancy. Ranulf's belated appearance had been greeted with understandable joy by his parents, but with unremitting jealousy by his sister. Age and subsequent separation had done nothing to mellow her sentiments towards him.

Sir Ranulf was endowed with dark colouring, as Bianca had suspected at the Green Dragon, but his sister's hair was so black as to look unnatural with its almost blue lights. However, it certainly was not so, and neither had guile nor artifice ever been employed by Laetitia to improve her brown complexion and

51

thin lips, which were forever clamped in disapproval for one reason or another. However, her dark eyes were remarkably fine and, had any warmth or *joie de vivre* ever been allowed to reach them, could have quite transformed the rest of her face. Ranulf had never witnessed any such transformation, and it was clearly unlikely that he was going to do so now.

"We arrived here only three days ago, but it seems an *age*, so distressing and altogether unpleasant has our visit proved . . . The uproar has been *prodigious*" (here her brother raised a disbelieving eyebrow), "and has severely injured Arthur's nerves—and my own, I may add, although I do not regard that . . . And the whole, I collect, can be laid at your door!" she flung at him with relish.

"*I*? Come now, Letty, what miff-maff is this? Uproar, *here*? Don't tell me mama has taken to wresting a tune from that abominable Egyptian lyre again —that is uproar indeed, I would agree."

But Laetitia treated this frivolity with the contempt it deserved. "You will not deny, I trust, that it was at your instigation that this brat—*whoever he may be*—" she interpolated heavily, "was foisted upon mama?"

Sir Ranulf struck his forehead with the palm of his hand. "Ah! I quite forgot—the boy, of course!" But he was remembering now and with a stab of guilt, not to mention a sense of foreboding; since that sobbing woman with Mrs Chart must have been none other than his governess . . .

"How like a man," Laetitia said sneeringly, "to be generous on other people's behalf, and then forget all about it. However, even you seem to have excelled yourself on this occasion."

Sir Ranulf did not know how the presence of the boy had come to slip his mind so completely; it was true that the arrangements concerning him had been made before he met with Lord Rishworth, but that was no excuse. His annoyance with himself made him speak harshly. "Damn it, Letty, this is my house and mama raised not the slightest objection to his staying here for a while in the care of a governess. Indeed, I thought she seemed to welcome the prospect of a little youthful company and vivacity."

His sister snorted loudly. "We have had more than our fill of youthful vivacity, brother dear, and the little brute has now deprived us of his company: not that *I* can view that with anything other than the greatest approbation, but it has wholly overset mama and thrown this Miss Hibbert into the strongest hysterics."

A most disagreeable feeling was now laying hold of Sir Ranulf. "Are you telling me that Gordon has disappeared?"

"I am." Laetitia was so pleased to tell him this that she almost smiled.

"Good God! *When*? What is being done about it?"

After receiving this intelligence, all thoughts of changing for dinner—even dinner itself—were banished from his mind. For nothing must be allowed to happen to Gordon whilst he was in his charge. Letty was right for once: he had been appallingly careless to leave the child's welfare in the hands of others, even for a few days. But it had simply never occurred to him that any ill could befall Gordon at Thrinby Hall.

"I will go to mama first," he murmured, striding abruptly past Laetitia. His travel-weariness seemed to have disappeared in the face of this crisis he had returned to. "Then I must set up a search before darkness falls. Thank heaven it is July and not January . . ."

Four

Whilst Lady Malvina was from home her spouse
lapsed quickly into the comfortable habit of not
changing for dinner; and the two girls, after enduring
a surfeit of dressing-up in London, were equally glad
to take the opportunity of less formal attire. So,
when Isabella went up to her room to change, after
paying calls upon several of their village acquaintance whom she had not seen for months, it was simply to put off a crumpled muslin morning dress and
don a fresh one. Their lady's maid, Miss Teign, had
remained with Isabella and Bianca in Town to the
end of their stay, but had now joined Lady Malvina
at Hippolita's home near Harrogate. Consequently,
Isabella's bedchamber had been left undisturbed
since her sister placed the note there. It was still
propped against the looking-glass on her dressing-ta-
ble when it caught her attention.

She snatched it up at once, for Bianca had been
out riding in the park an uncommon length of time
and she was already experiencing a sense of unease
about her. A slight smile touched her features as she
read the words 'Good Samaritan', but this was

quickly erased at mention of Thrinby Hall and a *small persecuted boy*. Lord, what had she been up to? she wondered, alarm beginning to overtake her as she recalled the mysterious screams emanating from the Hall grounds the day before, and now began to associate them with this 'persecuted boy'. Had Bianca heard the cries again, and felt it incumbent upon her to brave the wrath of the Thrinbys and snatch the boy from their midst? Apart from the danger in which she might be placing herself from whatever evil influence was abroad at the Hall, Isabella could not imagine what their father would do upon hearing of *any* involvement with the Thrinby family.

Not pausing for further useless reflections, she flew from her room and down the stairs, past the various imperturbable stone figures in their niches, and on to the Great Hall to consult the immense and grotesquely carved grandfather clock there, flanked by two guardian suits of armour. In spite of hands shaped like mailed fists clutching lances, it kept remarkable good time, and stood at ten minutes past four o'clock. Dinner was served at five-thirty and so she had ample time before encountering her father to pay a call on the Thrinbys. There was no denying it was a far from unpleasant prospect—but if Bianca had made off with one of their number, however ill-used, they must be told before they summoned the parish constable. It was possible her sister had hidden the boy in one of their several buildings and ruins dotted about the park, but Isabella felt that if this were so she would surely have returned by now to tell her.

She flitted back up the stairs, past the unheeding statues again and back to her chamber. There she threw on a riding dress instead of a morning gown and left her room in such dreadful disorder as would have reduced the methodical Miss Teign to near apoplexy.

Whilst the stableboy saddled up her mama's horse for her—Isabella explaining as calmly as she was able that the gelding was in sore need of exercise—she tried to ferret out Bianca's earlier movements from him.

"Ay miss, Miss Bianca brought Dandy in not long after you left, and then within the half hour she goes off again—this time with portmanteau an' all." He grinned placidly. "I remember I said, joking like, was she going off to see the new bab—but she didn't say."

"Portmanteau?" Isabella's voice almost cracked, but observing Tom's growing curiosity she added: "Oh yes . . . I daresay she was taking it to the saddler in the village. There was a strap broken on it, I collect."

The stableboy looked affronted. "Beg pardon, miss, but that's plain daft! Us could've mended it easy right 'ere. Jack can stitch a treat, you knows that."

"Yes, I do, of course, but perhaps Bianca had forgotten," she returned feebly. "Hand me up, Tom, if you please, and I'll put this fellow through his paces."

But the now puzzled lad glanced up at the burnished sky, and frowned at the young mistress. "Think on, miss, it's still a bit hot, like."

"Yes, yes, don't fret! You know me better than that, I hope."

Tom then watched her urge her mount out of the

yard at the liveliest gait imaginable: he rubbed a hand on the sleeve of his smock-like white overall in a mystified fashion. It was high time, he reckoned, that her ladyship came home and took them two lasses in hand a bit . . .

As might be expected there was no well-worn short cut from the Priory to Thrinby Hall, and Isabella had first to ride to the public highway and then about half a mile further on before the main Thrinby lodge-gate was reached. Perhaps she would not get beyond the lodge-keeper: who, for all she knew, might have standing instructions to keep all the de Hyvilles at bay. Her papa had never installed a lodge-keeper in their own vast medieval style gatehouse, as it possessed only arrow slits for windows, and men objected to occupying it; but if a keeper had been there she felt certain that no Thrinbys would have been admitted under any circumstances whatsoever.

That thought depressed her still more as the horse beneath her stretched its limbs to a full gallop. The road then curved in front of her, and it was with very mixed feelings that she rounded the curve and saw the impressive iron gates of her destination standing wide open before her. And, no sooner had she steeled herself to enter them, than a curricle and pair swung into sight in the drive beyond and bore down upon her at a cracking pace.

The driver she recognized at once as Sir Ranulf, despite only one previous brief meeting. She raised her whip hand in an endeavour to halt him outside the gates, but he mistook that gesture as a greeting and merely vouchsafed her a grim-faced nod in response. The gates were already being closed behind him and so, rather helplessly, Isabella reined the chestnut around and set off after the curricle. It was a narrow road but they were on a fairly straight part of it, and she soon drew level with him.

"What the devil?" Sir Ranulf cried out, with every sign of displeasure; although he did not slacken his pace.

"Forgive me!—but you are Sir Ranulf Thrinby, are you not? I should very much like to talk with you." She had to raise her voice above the noise of the carriage and felt at a considerable disadvantage; nonetheless, she thought it preferable to be without the Thrinby gates rather than within them.

"It is really not convenient. I am in a great hurry, as you can see." But he took his eyes briefly off the road and his pace slowed a little more. "Whom have I the pleasure of addressing?"

The tone patently lacked sincerity and Isabella felt convinced that a mention of her name was all that was necessary to send him bowling on his way: but there was no help for it and she told him.

"Ah!—I suspected as much," he replied, though without discernible malice, and pulled up his horses all standing. "Were you abroad in the village today, perhaps, Miss de Hyville?"

His sudden stop took her by surprise, and she halted her mount a little ahead of the curricle pair. Looking back, she began: "Yes, I—"

"Then did you perchance see a small boy about seven years old, possibly in the company of a young lady?"

"No, but I—"

Again he cut across her, his brief interest fading.

"No, I suppose it was not very likely." He urged his horses forward again. "You must excuse me now, ma'am . . ."

"Wait!" the note of sheer desperation in her voice penetrated even his distracted mind, and he hesitated. "*I* wanted to ask *you* about a small boy too! It may be the same one—I think he may be with my sister."

"With *your sister*?" he echoed with incredulity. "You are telling me it was your sister at the Green Dragon?"

"*The Green Dragon*!" It was Isabella's turn to be incredulous.

"Yes, not two hours ago, and fool that I was I helped the pair of them on their way with my own chaise! Where were they bound? And what sort of rig is your sister running, in heaven's name, can you tell me that?"

That Sir Ranulf's patience was fast running out was quite clear—and small wonder, thought Isabella, as she told him that she knew nothing of the affair beyond the meagre contents of Bianca's note. Even now she naturally forebore to mention what that missive had alleged regarding the persecution of a minor at Thrinby Hall.

Sir Ranulf rasped: "Samaritan? What can she mean? Forgive me for asking, but is your sister a trifle touched in the head, ma'am?"

"Of course she is not!" Isabella retorted, with an indignant flash of her eyes; although she was beginning to wonder something of the sort herself. "In any event, why did you not apprehend the boy if you saw him?" she countered, feeling that everyone about her seemed to have taken sudden leave of their senses.

"The lady had some Banbury tale to tell about her nephew absconding from school, which, if I had had my wits about me I would have recognised as havy cavy in the extreme—for who ever heard of schooling in July? But in fact I paid scant heed to either of them, being too exhausted at that time by far . . ."

Isabella had no difficulty in believing him on that head: he still looked fagged to death. And perhaps he had not actually set eyes upon the boy at the inn. "You are going to the Green Dragon now, I collect?"

"Are you able to suggest somewhere better?" he asked caustically.

She bit her lip. "No, I wish that I could."

"So do I, for I know I shall discover little enough when I get there. But I must be on my way—they have several hours start, wherever they are bound."

"I'll come with you!"

He cast her a look of withering contempt. "I think not. In my view the de Hyvilles have caused more than enough mischief for one day. Good-day to you, ma'am."

Isabella, quite dashed down by the severity of this remark, and more bewildered than ever by the turn of events, let the curricle go ahead of her and disappear from sight.

*   *   *

Sir Ranulf did not look back. Interfering females! he fulminated to himself. Lord knew what maggot had got into the first girl's head to make off with the child like that . . . His mother had been able to throw lit-

61

tle light upon Gordon's vanishing—except to describe the boy and make him realize that he had in fact seen him earlier himself. The governess, it seemed, was woefully inadequate to her task and exercised little control over her charge, who was clearly (and this came as no great surprise to him) a pickle of the first order and possessed of the utmost alacrity of falling into scrapes. Perhaps Gordon had abducted Miss de Hyville, he chuckled grimly to himself: certainly she had been experiencing difficulty in controlling him when he had first come upon the pair.

The half-smile was completely swept from his face as he recalled the prospect now before him; if the younger Miss de Hyville had no intention of returning home that day—and it would be folly to believe a single word she had said—he did not know where he would begin to look for her. Besides, he must not lose sight of the fact that Gordon was the one who mattered. He could make no sense of the girl's part in it, and suddenly wondered if there was some fiendish plot afoot to kidnap the lad. For it would not come as a total surprise to him if certain people sought the custody of Gordon for their own ends; but what really had him grassed was how they had discovered his whereabouts so soon.

Abandoning that train of thought for the moment, he tried to remember something—nay, anything—about his neighbours, the de Hyvilles. His father had spoken of the old boy invariably in the most derogatory terms imaginable, saying he was a pretentious mushroom, and an archduke of surpassing oddity, who had despoiled the Priory and its park with his monstrous creations; his most outrageous stroke of neighbourly aggravation being the erection of 'that damned spy tower', as his parent had called the belvedere, and which was conspicuous from almost every vantage point in Thrinby Hall.

However, nothing could be more remote from Gordon and his connexions than the Priory sort of people, and that the de Hyvilles should have designs upon him was scarcely credible. That left only the possibility of a hereditary mental disorder, but even his father had never gone so far as to call Sir John mad; and, provoking and calamitous as the daughters of the house appeared to be, he supposed it would be premature to judge them as specifically deranged at this stage . . .

He turned on to the Harrogate road, springing his horses on the better surface but keeping an alert eye for the chaise he had so recklessly dismissed earlier. If only he could speak to the postboys now, it would tell him all he needed to know to run the fugitives to ground. But unless Miss de Hyville had merely put her captive into other hands and returned in the chaise to collect her mount from the Green Dragon, it was in the highest degree likely that the postboys would drive back to their posting-house at Ripon. In any event he would discover what he could from the landlord—and with rather more tenacity than before, he thought dourly. If he still drew a blank, he would be compelled to drive on to Ripon himself in an attempt to run the postboys to earth: *if* they were not already there and embarking upon fresh journeys, he reflected with another surge of frustration, and whipped his horses faster, although it went against the pluck to overtax his cattle thus in the heat.

The Green Dragon finally hove in sight beyond the animals' heads, and only a farm tumbril of hay and two solitary gaitered riders had he passed en route. There was no tollgate on that stretch of road, so confirmation of earlier traffic along it with a gatekeeper was impossible. However, he would soon pass through a turnpike on the road beyond the inn, and that might yield some information, he thought, clutching at straws.

He drove swiftly and skillfully into the inn yard, despite his now returned weariness, and jumped down calling: "House, there!"

The Green Dragon, which was not much more than a village pot-house, had seen some uncommonly stirring events that day, what with a runaway schoolboy in the charge of a devastatingly pretty aunt barely out of the schoolroom herself, guineas tossed about like groats, and a fine gentleman who had condescended to say theirs was the best home-brew he had tasted in many a long ride: all this excitement, together with the heat of the afternoon, had pushed the inmates without exception into the arms of Morpheus.

Sir Ranulf, exasperated at this soporific reception, led his horses towards the stables. There, he found an ostler recumbent upon a pile of hay, and shook him none too gently back to sensibility. It took him some further time to learn from the bemused fellow that the chaise had not come back, and that the young lady's mount was still stabled there. He gave precise instructions as to the care required for his own horses and then strode across the yard in search of the landlord.

His progress was checked abruptly by a motionless horse and rider. "Good God!"

In other circumstances, Isabella might have allowed herself a certain satisfaction to have so thoroughly confounded this glumpish block who had brushed aside her help with such contempt; but since her one concern was to find Bianca, to that end she was ready to be as ingratiating as needs be to Sir Ranulf. But it was not going to be easy, and she bit back the retort which sprang to her lips when he demanded roughly: "What in heaven's name are you doing here now?"

"I beg your pardon," she said with dignity, and dismounting in haste before he could assist her—although that did not seem likely, judging from his formidable aspect. "I believe I may be able to help you to find the runaways."

This drew a look of the deepest scepticism. "Indeed? I thought you professed to be quite ignorant of their whereabouts."

"I have had time to think as I rode along. There is only one place in this direction that Bianca would know, where she could be sure of a cordial reception in the circumstances." Here her audience raised a dark eyebrow, but she continued undaunted: "My elder sister's residence, which lies this side of Harrogate."

She was unwilling to divulge the name of the house to him because she guessed he would insist upon riding there alone; and she hesitated to think what might happen if she were wrong in her surmise and her mama, and possibly Hippolita's husband also, were faced with a finally infuriated Sir Ranulf

65

Thrinby. By now she was half-convinced that Bianca *must* have taken leave of her senses to go jiggeting about the countryside in this fashion. She felt a pang of guilt herself, though, for she suspected that her own recent advice on offering a helping hand to those in need must have been somehow at the root of this ridiculous escapade.

"Are you sure of this?" he asked her.

"Of course I am not *sure*! I cannot make one jot of sense of the whole affair, but if it was my sister you saw here this afternoon—"

"We may at least be able to establish that now. Do you go and look at the horse that was left here—the ostler will show you. I will hold yours for you."

Isabella returned to him a few moments later with her emotions in shaken order: seeing Dandy abandoned in a strange stable had served to bring home the gravity of the situation. "Yes, that is Bianca's mount," she almost whispered.

"So, there is nothing for it but to drive the best part of the way to Harrogate, I collect. In that case, as soon as I have ascertained that the landlord can throw no further light on these wretched runaways, I will be off." He handed the bridle back to Isabella and headed for the inn's entrance, calling: "House! House, damn you!" in tones of the utmost brusquerie.

Isabella was now at a complete stand: never in her life had she been faced with such a quandary. The dinner-hour at the Priory must be fast approaching, and if neither she nor Bianca was present, even their easy-going father was liable to experience some degree of alarm; and then, if he should discover that the Thrinbys lay at the root of their absence . . . No, it did not bear contemplation—but then nor did the prospect of Sir Ranulf confronting her mama at Flaxby House fill her with anything but the direst foreboding. Oh, if only she knew *where* that wretched girl had gone—and why . . .

By the time the truculent figure of Sir Ranulf was advancing upon her again across the cobbles, she had decided that all things considered, it would be wiser for her to return home and allay the suspicions of her father. Sir Ranulf was clearly bent upon finding the child, come what might, and she had informed him of the only possible place where Bianca could have taken him. She felt, too, that her further presence—assuming he would tolerate it at all—could only serve to aggravate his already hostile feelings towards her. She hoped he would not be too severe upon Bianca if he succeeded in tracking her down, but that would have to be left to fate. Now was certainly not the time to attempt to plead her sister's case.

He addressed her without preamble: "I can learn nothing further than that the chaise took the Harrogate road—which circumstance points, if not very conclusively, to their destination being your sister's home, as you thought. *Boy!*" he called aside, in the direction of the stables. "The curricle—at once, if you please!" Turning back to Isabella, he said in tones almost as peremptory: "Stable your mount here, ma'am, and I will take you up beside me for the rest of the journey."

In dismay Isabella exclaimed: "No, no, I cannot, Sir Ranulf! It is imperative I return—"

"I do not deny that I have had my fill of meddling females today," he interrupted her in a dangerous voice, "but you chose to follow me thus far and it now suits me that you should accompany me to your sister's house—where, I may say, I am likely to cut a very odd figure if your conjecture is wrong. Indeed, I can hardly like the prospect if you are in the right of it. You do, I suppose, know the best road there?"

"Yes, of course I—but—"

"Good. Then we will be on our way. Come, there is no time to be lost! God only knows where this wild-goose chase will lead me in the end," he declared in disgust, as he walked off towards the harassed ostler who was bringing out the grays.

There was nothing for it: she realized that she would have to go with him, in his present mood; and to be honest she did want to be there—*if* they found Bianca. However, she was determined at least to send a message to her father, setting his mind at rest. "Sir Ranulf—can you oblige me with a sheet from your pocketbook and a pencil?" she ventured, fairly certain that this hedge tavern would provide no such refinements.

He looked around from adjusting the harness. "Dash it, this is no time to be writing letters!"

"I *must* send a short note to my papa, explaining . . . everything."

"Well, ma'am, if you can do that in a few lines, then you must surely deserve the opportunity," he said, with a sardonic gleam in his eye but drawing out the requisite items from a tail-pocket.

Resting the pocket book against the flank of her horse, she scribbled unsteadily: 'Dear Papa, Pray do not be angry but Bianca and I had a sudden notion to ride over to see how Polly goes on. I daresay we may stay overnight if it should prove convenient. Yr. loving daughter, Isabella.'

She tore out the page of stiff expensive paper with some feeling of guilt. "I'm sorry I have had to spoil your book," she told him, handing it back.

"Oh, please do not regard *that*! If *that* were all . . ." He let the words hang eloquently in the air.

She was partway across the yard with her note when she checked and led her horse back to Sir Ranulf again. "I do beg your pardon, sir," she faltered, "but if I am to despatch a messenger I must reward him. Do you—could you—oblige me with some money?"

"For pity's sake are we *never* to start? Besides, I thought the de Hyvilles always travel with a crock of gold about their persons. There," he added, placing a coin forcibly in her hand, "that should suffice."

She wondered herself if a shilling would be enough, but was in no position to quibble. "Thank you, thank you very much . . ." She led her animal away to the stables once again and concluded her arrangements with the increasingly interested ostler; such comings and goings he'd not seen in many a long day.

Sir Ranulf was waiting in the curricle with his arms folded repressively across his chest when she returned, but he leaned over and handed her up into the seat beside him. She hardly had time to reflect what a superior vehicle it was, before they were proceeding along the Harrogate road, and she was clutching at her hat in the breeze which had sprung up.

After a while she tentatively broke the heavy silence between them. "Sir Ranulf, what did you mean by a crock of gold just now?"

Without taking his eyes from the road ahead, he told her: "Merely that your sister threw the landlady of the Green Dragon into a rare pucker by casting guineas before her for a jug of lemonade."

"Oh *no! Guineas!*" This threw a new light altogether upon her sister's activities. Could she be planning to go to Harrogate to take the stage there, perhaps escorting the boy to some distant destination of his own suggesting? Needless to say she did not care to voice these new apprehensions to her companion, but she was prey to still further misgivings when he said presently:

"Now, you had best tell me the quickest road to your sister's. I am anxious to put an end to this affair as soon as may be. It is past five o'clock now and time is short if I am to be home by nightfall." She noticed that he did not include herself in his later plans, but then realized that there would not be room in the curricle for Bianca, the boy, and herself, to return together. "I do not scruple to say that if you are incorrect in your assumption it will go ill with you both," he continued chillingly. "For, should anything happen to that boy whilst he is in my care, it will be bellows to mend with me—and I do not jest, Miss de Hyville."

Isabella could see that he did not.

Five

When Bianca left the Green Dragon, some three
hours before Isabella and Sir Ranulf were to arrive
there, she sank back on to the shabby squabs of the
hired chaise and breathed a sigh of relief: she was out
of that beastly scorching sun, Gordon was sitting
quietly beside her unable, she hoped devoutly, to
cause any more mischief, and within the hour she
would be able to lay her problems before someone else.

She congratulated herself upon her guile in not dis-
closing the destination before all and sundry at the
inn; and after they had been running it in the chaise
for ten minutes she pulled the checkstring to halt the
vehicle. Then she told the postboy on the box: "I
wish to go to Ashbeck now. It is a turning off to the
right on this road, a few miles ahead—there is a finger
post."

"Yes, miss, we knows it," the driver replied, in the
superior tones of the master-hand whose abilities are
being thrown into doubt.

Bianca was glad to hear the way was familiar to
him, for she was none too certain of it herself. It was
true she had kept a particular look out for the turn-

71

ing, when they had travelled back from London only days before, wishing to know more precisely where Mr Carleton Amersham lived; but beyond that side road, she had no notion how far they might have to travel. Again she addressed the postboy.

"Ashbeck village?—eight or nine miles—give or take a mile or two," he qualified hastily, in case he should wish to adjust the charges later. The gentry cove's generous offer of their services to this passenger, dimber mort though she undoubtedly was, had not pleased them overmuch: females on their own generally meant trouble sooner or later. He exchanged a weary wink with the other postboy seated on the off-side leader.

"So we should be there within the hour, then?" Bianca persisted.

"*If* we can get on, miss, yes."

"Oh yes, of course, thank you." She slid the window shut, and was tumbled back to her seat as the postboys used their whips and the equipage lurched forward again.

When she had straightened her beaver hat she tried to apply herself to a little mental arithmetic to ascertain the likely charges for the journey, on the information she had acquired at the inn and this latest estimate of the distance to be covered. At one-and-twopence a mile for each horse, that would be four-and-eightpence a mile; so, say ten miles to Ashbeck . . . Goodness, she thought, forty shillings at least, and with eighty pence it would be—

"Yee-ee-ee-ee!" Gordon shouted, as the chaise gathered speed and the hedgerows seemed to fly past.

He was kneeling on the seat with his nose pressed to the cold glass.

Bianca winced but did not chide him, merely leaning forward to check that the door on his side of the carriage was securely locked. She returned to her anxious calculations. Two pounds, six shillings and eightpence, she finally totalled: and then that must be doubled if she was to return to the Green Dragon later—and there would be tips to be paid. Lord! Five pounds at the very least would be needed, so it was just as well that she had brought all her money with her. Whether or not she would have to pay for the postboys' return journey to their posting-house she did not know, and she was certainly not going to ask that horrid man on the box. However, that was something else Mr Amersham would be able to tell her when she arrived at Ashbeck, she thought. For a moment she was annoyed that the gentleman who had provided the chaise should have had such expensive tastes in travelling, for she reflected crossly that if there were only a pair of horses her costs would be halved; but her general sense of gratitude soon ousted these churlish feelings, and she sat back with a sigh and resolved to try and enjoy this unexpected journey at least to some degree.

From time to time she endeavoured to discover from Gordon a little more about himself, but she could learn nothing new except that he had evidently made a recent and much longer journey, presumably to Trinby Hall. After about an hour even his youthful energies flagged a little, and when his endless comments upon the passing scene suddenly ceased she saw that he was fast asleep. His expression of seraphic vulnerability then pierced her heart, and served to strengthen her determination to do all in her power to protect him from his tormentors.

He was clearly quite worn out by his adventures, for he slept all through their arrival at Ashbeck village, where noisy inquiries had to be made for the Amersham residence, and indeed was still asleep when the steps were let down for Bianca to alight at its main entrance.

Putting a finger to her lips, Bianca bade the postboys leave her 'nephew' undisturbed: she felt considerable relief at not having him in tow when she first approached the Amershams' front door. It was a pretty stone house with sash windows partly obscured by Virginia creeper; an unpretentious building of modest size set no more than twenty yards away from the road behind a low wall, and backed by a rookery of old elms.

Before she could tug at the bell a sash was raised above her head, to the right of the entrance, and Julia Amersham leaned out. "Who is that?—*Bianca*! . . . oh dear!" she exclaimed.

"Julia! Oh, I cannot tell you how glad I am to see you," Bianca called up to her friend in a voice breaking with emotion and distress. "I am so sorry to arrive unannounced, but I need your help quite *desperately*, you see . . ."

Julia's glance quickly took in the hired chaise, and the lounging postboys who were interested observers of this touching tableau. The child curled up in the corner of the carriage seat was not visible to her. "Oh dear," she said once again, and looked rather distracted. "This is dreadful—have you had the measles?"

"Measles?" echoed Bianca uncomprehendingly; her mind so full of her own concerns that she could not attend to anything outside them.

"Yes, we have measles in the house: three of my young brothers and two sisters, all quite full of it, I fear."

Understanding finally dawned. "Oh, the *measles*! Pooh, I had them ages ago! I do not regard that," Bianca told her blithely, still too taken up with herself to reflect that she might not be a wholly welcome visitor to a family nursing five youthful invalids. "May I come in? I must talk with you—alone," she added darkly, and with a pointed look at the postboys.

In a residence the size of this one, housing a family of Amersham proportions, a private conversation was always liable to interruption: at the moment it was out of the question for Julia even to attempt it. "I shall come down, if you will wait a minute," she said resignedly.

The door was soon opened and Julia appeared. Almost at once she cried: "Oh, lord, my apron!" and snatched in annoyance at the strings. "There now—they've knotted! Could you oblige me, Bianca?" She turned around.

"Oh—yes—surely." Bianca hastily peeled off her gloves. "But why ever are you wearing this?" She had never before seen anyone but a housemaid in such a practical starched garment.

"Looking after five sick children can be a messy business, you know," Julia retorted, her temper not at its best by this time.

75

"Yes, I suppose so," agreed Bianca vaguely; who until that day had not had the care of even one child, sick or otherwise.

Julia thanked her for releasing her and cast the offending apron aside. "Come, let us walk this way," she suggested, guiding Bianca away from the post-boys' avid curiosity. "Now, pray, tell me, what is the trouble?" she asked kindly, and with commendable restraint.

"I've no wish to put you about," Bianca murmured somewhat belatedly. "I—I just wondered if Mr Carleton was home?"

Julia now shot her a look of acute alarm. Her mind swiftly marshalled the facts of this matter: here was Bianca in some deep trouble, come to seek out *her* brother, in a hired chaise and with no companion or even a maid . . . My God, she thought, it cannot be! She knew Bianca had been mightily taken with Carleton, of course, but she did not think he had given her the least encouragement, let alone . . . She ran an apprehensive eye over Bianca's figure and observed that she was remarkably well-clad for travelling on a hot summer's day—and a trifle dowdy, almost as if she were trying to escape notice. "Carleton?" she repeated stupidly, as though she had never heard the name before.

"Yes, if I could just have a word with him I'm persuaded he will know how to go on in a case of this nature—especially after what happened in Town. For I have no idea, I really don't!" Bianca wailed in rising agitation. "You see, there is *no one else* I can turn to . . ."

"No, no, I suppose not," Julia answered faintly, her

round homely face already a little drawn as a result of several disturbed nights and now becoming paler still. "But I fear he did not travel home with us," she continued, watching her friend's face very closely as she gave her this bad news. "I am not sure we even have his present direction."

Bianca, who had secretly been thinking that this escapade at least made an excuse for her to visit Mr Amersham, now said in a desolated voice: "Oh . . . that never occurred to me."

Julia, now foreseeing this was likely to be a protracted, not to say delicate talk, asked her: "Would it not be sensible to send the postboys to the stables?" She had remembered that luckily their groom was not, for once, absent on an errand to fetch the doctor, or to collect medicaments from the apothecary.

"Oh yes, I am sure it would be! I have never hired a chaise before on my own account, and as you see I have no notion what to do . . . thank you."

Julia hurried over to the postboys and told them that ale would be forthcoming from the kitchen if they went to the rear of the house: she only hoped that cook was not in the throes of preparing one of her nourishing broths for the invalids. The men needed no second bidding, and quickly drove the chaise round to the stables.

"There now," Julia said brightly, returning to the visitor, but becoming momently more harrassed as she thought that her presence would soon be missed indoors with only Betty, the housemaid, in attendance upon the sickroom. Her mama was trying to snatch some rest after all the demands made upon her strength over the past days. It was very unfortunate that their nursemaid had been dismissed, in the cause of retrenchment, only a week before the measles had struck. "Shall we go inside for a while?" she murmured, with her own concerns uppermost in her mind. But then she recalled her friend's condition, and supposed that it might be wiser for her—in particular—not to pass into a house of sickness; besides which, there was less chance of their being overheard outside. So she said hastily: "There is a nice seat by the path, though, and I should not mind a breath of air myself if you do not object?"

"No, I should prefer the fresh air—you see I must think of the boy," Bianca confided.

"A boy!" Julia exclaimed, her eyes bulging with astonishment: *how could she be sure of the sex of her child*!—though it was said that some could—but to speak of it all in such *casual style*!

"Yes, I would not want to expose him to the measles, and I daresay he hasn't had it yet, being very young."

At this point a maggot of doubt entered Julia's tired brain; although she felt it was no longer capable of making sense of anything. She sat down heavily on the garden seat. "What boy is this, Bianca?" she asked, in the quiet and humouring tones of one dealing with a dangerous imbecile and regarding her with wariness.

"Well, that is part of the difficulty, you see I don't really know," came the unreassuring reply. "But he has been most *dreadfully maltreated*—such bruises you've never seen! Poor little lamb, so severe was his suffering that he was quite set upon running away to the gypsies. You do see I had to aid him, don't you?"

she appealed to her dumbfounded audience. "And so I brought him here."

"Here?" Julia echoed, scanning the garden with a distraught eye.

"Yes, I thought perhaps he could stay with you, at least while your brother decided what should be done for him—I know he is so kind . . ."

Julia still understood very little of all this, but, as it seemed her original surmise had been mercifully wide of the mark, she thought it was high time to register a protest. "You must see it is out of the question! Carleton isn't here—although what *he* has to say to anything, I do not know. And even if he were at hand, we would still have the measles. Oh, dear, where *is* the boy?" She looked wildly about her again. "He must not be permitted to enter the house!"

"Of course not—don't fret, he is fast asleep in the chaise. The poor little fellow is quite worn out," Bianca replied in an abstracted fashion, for she was only now beginning to perceive just how disastrously this visit had turned out.

"Why could you not keep him at your house?" Julia asked; with good reason, she thought, considering how much more comfortable were the de Hyvilles' circumstances than their own.

"But that would not serve at all. The boy claims to come from Thrinby Hall, you see—and so papa would be bound to send him back at once."

If Julia thought this an admirable notion, she commendably refrained from saying so. Instead she now devoted her efforts to disentangling herself from the whole affair, which she regarded as an unfair burden on top of all her others. "Well, I suppose it does sound very regrettable, but you do understand how impossible it is for me to offer you help, placed as we are?" With a big effort she summoned up a smile and rose to her feet. "Had you found us all in a state of robust health, matters would have been different, of course. But as it is—" She shrugged.

Bianca stood up also, beginning to quiver all over. She did not know *what* she was going to do now. "Yes, yes, I know you would help if it lay in your power." She uttered a few more words of mechanical thanks.

Her demeanour was so very woebegone that Julia felt it incumbent upon her to apologise again for not being more hospitable. "I know it does seem beyond everything to be unable even to offer you refreshments, but—"

"Oh no! I do not wish anything for myself," Bianca declared in a stronger voice. "It is only for the boy, you see . . . I *cannot* abandon him to his cruel fate, Julia. I declare I should be a monster even to think of doing so." Tears showed in her eyes and one ran pathetically down her cheek.

Julia, who had always had to contend with a host of boisterous younger brothers and sisters, the hopeful progeny of a now ailing mother and a far from prosperous sire, had never been able to indulge the kind of excessive sensibility of the sort Bianca was wont to display—for she had noticed this lachrymose tendency in her friend even in London. But she curbed her impatience, saying: "Are you quite sure he *is* ill-treated, my dear? Some small boys have a capacity for untruths, you know, which is quite staggering—and for running away too, I may say! Little Ger-

80

vase has twice absconded, and on the first occasion, why, he was no bigger than a bee's knee!"

"Of course I am sure! You forget I have seen his injuries!"

Julia still looked a trifle sceptical. "Perhaps he has just taken a tumble," she suggested. "They do sustain the most alarming looking contusions sometimes.—Or possibly done battle with another boy?"

"Well, thank you, Julia," Bianca said coldly, holding out her hand in a dignified manner. "If you will be kind enough to summon my carriage I will be on my way now."

"Yes, of course." Julia clasped the proffered hand, scarcely knowing by this time whether to laugh or cry.

When her friend had gone back inside, Bianca paced the gravel drive in great agitation while she waited for the chaise, racking her brains for what further directions she could give to the postboys. Her resources would barely cover her return to the Green Dragon; and if she took that course she felt it would be to admit total public defeat. She had not forgotten that her sister Hippolita was placed not far away from here, and in the ordinary way might well have turned to her for assistance; but, with the baby no more than a few days old, and her mama there too (who would perhaps not look any more warmly on a Thrinby boy than her father), she decided that there was no hope for her in that quarter.

She heard the chaise coming round the house and realized there was nothing for it: she would have to return home and face censure and blame—all for nothing . . .

The postboy riding postilion dismounted and

pulled down the steps for her, looking a good deal more cheerful than he had upon arrival: the pair had been regally entertained by the bored Amersham groom, who rarely saw a stranger. But his look of complacency was swiftly removed when he pulled open the chaise door. "Lor . . . he's gawn!"

"Gone—what do you mean?" Bianca almost over-balanced as she jumped up on the bottom step, craning her neck to see round the postboy's broad shoulders.

He continued to gape at the empty seat. "He was there, miss, asleep like . . ."

"I *know* he was, you dolt, but he isn't now, is he? Pray go straightway and look in the stables—he dotes upon horses and I daresay you will find him there!"

Julia, who had unwisely chosen that moment to appear again at the bedroom window to wave her visitor goodbye, asked with some trepidation: "Is anything wrong?"

"The boy has now vanished from the chaise," Bianca told her in a faint, choking voice.

"Oh dear . . ." Julia lamented yet again. "I do hope he has not crept into the house unobserved."

Bianca was now quite speechless over this new anxiety. The postboy soon returned empty-handed, and Julia said crossly: "I will search the house myself. Do you continue looking about the garden."

Bianca and one postboy then wandered about the not very extensive grounds, leaving the other fellow in charge of the harnessed horses. All three of them began calling the boy's name, but Bianca knew it would be fruitless: he had run away as he had said he would.

Some ten minutes later Julia came again to the window and announced that no strange boy was within; also that she had taken the precaution of locking the doors against his trying to enter.

"What *am I going to do*?" Bianca wailed up to her long-suffering friend.

"I think you had best repair to the parish constable and enlist his help," Julia said firmly. "I expect the boy will hide in a barn, or in the new-mown hay roundabout. He sounds much too young to stray far afield on his own, and if he is seen by a *responsible person* he is sure to be turned over to the constable." She then proceeded to give directions to the postboys where they might discover that officer. "Content yourself, my dear, that once he is found he will be delivered into the constable's charge with all despatch." And with this brisk assurance she bade Bianca farewell, closing the window with a gesture of finality which brought another rush of tears to the eyes of her sensitive unwanted guest.

Bianca clambered blindly into the chaise, which seemed horribly empty and alien to her without the boy. She sat with her gloved hands clenched together, and tried to force herself to think of what she must tell the constable. Wholly unused to making decisions, and to the whole ordeal of traveling on her own, a sort of despairing panic gripped her: she just could not face any more unfamiliar people or places! Apart from this final blow she had sustained over the boy, she was also haunted by the thought of poor

Dandy waiting for her at the Green Dragon—doubtless hungry and unwatered. Oh, it was all *impossible!* Besides, she reflected hopelessly, what could she say to the parish constable that would make the least particle of sense? She did not even know the boy's full name, nor, for sure, where he lived. And from Julia's unfeeling response (although she was sure Carleton would have been everything sympathetic) she had apprehended that her own role in the affair was not likely to be viewed with universal approval or understanding. An upholder of the law, like the constable, was bound to regard her story with suspicion—why, he might even think she had kidnapped the child . . .

The postboys were now in a great hurry to complete their eccentric mission, and consequently the chaise jounced and jolted along the rough country lanes. When Bianca again raised her wet eyes and looked out of the window she felt giddy and faint: she had no idea of the time, but apart from a ladylike sip of lemonade at the inn she had partaken of no nourishment at all since breakfast. She ached to be home again.

Trying to review her actions in the best possible light, it occurred to her that she had not failed altogether in her aim to help Gordon. After all, since he had set his dear little heart upon escaping from those fiends at the Hall, by bringing him to Ashbeck she had at least ensured that he was at some remove from their pursuit. Besides, she thought, her line of reasoning growing still more confused, if someone did find him nearby, and hand him over to the constable, just as Julia had said—what need was there for *her* to see that formidable (and doubtless rough-mannered) person herself at all? Being a man, he would probably have more success in extracting information from Gordon than she had managed to . . .

Yes, if she were to return home at once, no one perhaps need know of this ill-starred enterprise—save for Isabella . . . Oh, how she now regretted leaving that tell-tale note! She would have to concoct some white lie or another to explain her long absence, but that would be as naught compared with facing the constable . . . She reached up to the checkstring before her resolution had time to falter.

The chaise took some while to grind to a halt. "Yes, miss?" the driver said, permitting himself a full measure of weary insolence.

"Return to the Green Dragon at once, if you please," Bianca called shrilly through the small window. "I choose not—I have decided not—that is, I think I *shall* not go to the parish constable!"

The fellow favoured her with a slow gap-toothed grin, and for a fearful moment Bianca thought he was going to defy her, but at last he said: "Ay, very well, miss. But I dunno where we shall find space enough to turn the team in, eh, Harry? It will add a tidy bit to the fare, miss and no mistake," he concluded more happily.

"Never mind that!" snapped Bianca, her nerves now on the full stretch. "The Green Dragon, as fast as maybe!"

The window slammed shut and the driver spat contemptuously into the ditch. Then he muttered over the horses' heads to his companion: "Well, knock me bandy! I told you, didn't I? Petticoats—be they tabbies or young 'uns—allus mean trouble—and don't never let nobody tell you no different!"

Six

Zach Webb, the turnpike keeper (once a postilion until he was crippled by a kick from an ill-tempered wheeler), found his toll-house small and oppressive after the open road, so in all but the most inclement weather he sat outside and waited for his customers to arrive.

In spite of the isolated position of the turnpike gate on the Richmond to Harrogate road, his work afforded him a unique insight into the comings and goings of the neighbourhood and beyond: an inveterate gossip, he relished this aspect of his occupation, and made it his business to collect every nugget of information that came his way.

That particular sunny afternoon, he squinted along the glaring surface of the road and spied a Harrogate-bound curricle approaching at a rattling pace. He hobbled across to open the gate, recognizing the Thrinby horses at once. But he was a little surprised to see Sir Ranulf back so soon that day—and now with a young lady beside him. Zach's immediate thought that this might be the next Lady Thrinby at last, was not entirely dispelled when he noticed their grim, tight-lipped expressions: just a lovers' tiff most likely, he decided, scanning the lady's face with his sharp little eyes to see if it were familiar. It was, and yet it wasn't . . . He fancied he had seen the girl before, but to his vexation he could not put a name to her.

Sir Ranulf had the sixpenny toll ready, and handed it abruptly down to the keeper. "Tell me, man, has a hired chaise and four been through—heading south?"

Sensing from the urgency of the gentleman's voice that this inquiry might prove both interesting and profitable, Zach rubbed his chin in a teasing way and replied: "Ay—ay, I reckons one may've done at that," although in fact his precise memory was imprinted with every detail of a day's traffic.

"Come now, Zach, you can do better than that, as everyone knows," Sir Ranulf snapped impatiently. "You greeted the postilion like a long-lost brother when he drove me through here earlier."

The fact that the gentleman should have remembered his name so appeased the vanity of the keeper that he told all he knew at once. " 'Course, sir, you puts it in my mind, now. Yes, Harry was back in under the two-hour: and carrying the most taking wench you ever set your peepers on. I recall I said to him, Harry I said—"

"And was there a boy too?" Sir Ranulf interrupted with a quelling gesture.

"There was, sir," agreed Zach, suitably chastened: he had just observed the young lady's blushes, and simultaneously known her as the taking wench's sister. He swallowed, relieved that his more pungent comments to Harry had not been repeated in full.

"And where were they bound for?"

Sir Ranulf sighed as that question hung unanswered, and reluctantly fingered a shilling from his pocket; although telling himself that he was ready to disburse gold with the reckless vulgarity of a de Hyville by this stage, if only the escapade could thereby be brought to a close.

But the keeper was genuinely unable to oblige him, due to no lapse of inquisitiveness on his part but merely the turn of events: he had been just about to ask Harry the destination of the vehicle when the fetching wench had rapped on the window; and Harry, raising his eyes expressively to the heavens, had gone on his way.

Sir Ranulf did not linger now, but tossed the coin to the ground at the keeper's feet. "Keep a look out for me in case that chaise, or its occupants, pass this way again."

"Ay, sir," chirruped Zachary, in his element to be so charged.

"Very little escapes that fellow's lively curiosity," Sir Ranulf observed soon afterwards to his companion, "so I must assume your sister was at pains to keep her direction a secret. Why should she do that, do you suppose, Miss de Hyville, if she were *not* bent on kidnapping the boy?"

Isabella had none of Bianca's delicate features, taking more after her rather ill-favoured mama, although mercifully she had been spared the crooked teeth. Now, her over-generous lips parted in sheer amazement as she stared at his grim profile. "*Kidnapped*? You are being quite absurd, sir, if I may say so! I will not suffer my sister to be maligned in this style! If you must know, Bianca was merely concerned to remove the boy from persecution," she was stung into revealing.

"Persecution?" Sir Ranulf scoffed. "What new flim-flam is this, for pity's sake?"

"Yes, persecution," Isabella said hotly, on her mettle now to defend Bianca from the strictures of this odious man. "It is idle to seek to deny it. I was with my sister only yesterday, in the belvedere which overlooks your land, and—"

"I know it well, believe me," he cut across her with a sneer, adding beneath his breath: "Damnable spy tower . . ."

But Isabella caught that, and was disconcerted for a moment by his vehemence. Then she said with dignity: "Yes, I think I would not dispute with you on that head. However, as I was about to say, it was from there that we both heard the most chilling screams coming from *your grounds*. Now, I have not the smallest doubt that that incident, in some way, is connected with Bianca's rescue of this wretched boy from his tormentors."

"For the love of heaven, at least spare me your Gothic tales, ma'am," he responded in his most crushing tones. "I vow that freakish house of yours has addled all your wits—still, it is not to be wondered at, I daresay."

Isabella had been prepared to be fair about their encroaching belvedere, but this was the outside of enough—to dismiss the Priory, her papa's dearest creation, as a freak! Incensed, she snapped: "You go too far, sir!"

"Perhaps," he admitted wearily, "but no one can

say I have not suffered severe provocation. Tell me, what has your sister done but *gone too far?*"

"I prefer to reserve my judgement until I hear her side of the story," Isabella told him. If only she knew who this wretched boy was, and in what relation he stood to Sir Ranulf to cause this degree of protective zeal—but this was scarcely the moment to inquire into such a delicate matter. Besides which it really was none of her concern, as no doubt, in his present mood, he would point out to her in no uncertain terms.

"Ah!" he exclaimed suddenly, cutting into his companion's dark musings. "*That*, if I mistake it not, is the elusive chaise approaching—and with the redoubtable Harry still astride the leader."

Isabella watched the shabby yellow carriage-and-four come swaying towards them, with a tight feeling in her chest: she could only pray that it still concealed both Bianca and the child.

After halting his own vehicle, Sir Ranulf waved down the chaise with his whip. "Step down, if you would, Miss de Hyville," he instructed her with a kind of angry civility. "I will discover what I can from the postboys—and whilst I am doing so I depend upon you to ensure that whoever is inside that equipage does not abscond."

Isabella's by now feverish anxiety made her only too eager to comply with his wishes, but nonetheless she walked towards the hired carriage with the greatest sense of misgiving. Then she recognized the pale, desperate face of her sister at the window and hastened her step. But she was not in time to prevent

Bianca throwing open the door and jumping down impulsively into the road.

It was a long drop from the chaise without the aid of steps: Bianca landed awkwardly, emitted an anguished cry, and sank on to the stony ground.

"Oh, do take care!" Isabella cried, seconds too late, then leaned down to help Bianca to her feet.

"*No*! I *cannot*!—Oh Bella, I do believe I've broken my ankle!" And acute pain, mingled with her relief at seeing a family face again, totally overcame the damsel's battered nerves, and she sobbed with abandon into her sister's shoulder as she knelt beside her.

While this unfortunate accident was taking place, Sir Ranulf had discovered the baffling intelligence that his young quarry was running loose in a village called Ashbeck, miles away; and so there was scant sympathy in his voice when he shouted down to the ladies: "Come now, there is no time for this affecting reunion! I must be on my way just as soon as I have had a few words with the cause of all this trouble! What *is* the girl doing *now*?" He sprang down to investigate, bidding Harry to control the curricle pair while he was off the seat. Whereupon the wiseacre postboy up on the box of the chaise gave his knowing grin at young Harry once again, and remarked: "Told you so, din' I?—trouble, allus trouble from Petticoats . . ."

When Sir Ranulf found that he was required to sympathise with the culprit instead of castigating her, it was all he could do to maintain even a degree of complaisance. However, annoyed with him though she was, Isabella had to own that he behaved with commendable restraint in the circumstances.

"Now, my darling, Sir Ranulf will lift you back into the chaise," she said presently; and at this, the poor sufferer opened her eyes wide and murmured in an altered voice: "You?—You are *Sir Ranulf?*"

At his instigation Isabella examined Bianca's injured foot as soon as they had encoached again. She pronounced it, in her lay opinion, to be unshattered though badly strained. Bianca seemed so stunned by the kind stranger's reappearance upon the scene as Sir Ranulf, that she bore the examination in stoical silence, much to Isabella's relief.

"It is plain that you must accompany your sister home now," Sir Ranulf addressed her with studied indifference. "But," he added, turning once more to the half-reclining Bianca, "before you set off again in this ill-fated chaise I must ask you to explain what you have been thinking of, gallivanting all over the countryside with a child you snatched from under the nose of his governess!"

"I did *not* snatch him!" returned Bianca, in a voice still inclined to be tearful but which gained strength from her rising indignation. "He *came* to me—a poor hungry little waif, covered in the most frightful bruises, and saying he was going off to join the gypsies. Well, if he preferred the horrid dirty gypsies to living at Thrinby Hall, I *knew* he must be telling the truth, don't you see?"

Sir Ranulf cast a look of despair at Isabella standing beside him. "You have no younger brothers, ma'am, I collect?"

Scarcely daring to meet his eyes, she murmured: "No, none, sir."

He grunted, turning back to Bianca. "And where,

pray, did you intend taking this miserable maltreated reckling? Surely you had a vacant priest's hole or refurbished catacomb at the Priory, where you could have comforted him until we were brought to justice?"

Bianca coloured a little but said stubbornly: "I can't tell you that."

"Such loyalty does you great credit, I do not doubt," Sir Ranulf told her with a sardonic emphasis, "but I have already learned from these good fellows here that he escaped your tender care while in Ashbeck: that means he may well be disporting with the gypsies before sundown."

"Ashbeck!" now exclaimed Isabella, who had still assumed her sister had left the boy with Hippolita. "The *Amershams*? Oh, you *didn't* draw them into this bumblebath, did you?"

Bianca nodded and sniffed. "Yes, but it was no use —they have the measles."

Isabella said: "The what?" and Sir Ranulf gave a mirthless snort of laughter. "Ha! I see! You added spots to the bruises before you sent the boy to join the gypsies!"

"Of course not—Julia will let nobody into her precious house," Bianca said moodily.

"Julia?—no, never mind . . . I gain nothing from this exchange, and realise that it is folly to try," Sir Ranulf declared, his hand squeezing the handle of the chaise door as though he would dearly like it to be Bianca's neck. "However, I assure you you haven't heard the end of this matter, whatever the outcome. And I think even you must be aware that the consequences may be dire if I fail to find the child before

94

dark." With a curt nod to Isabella, and an injunction to them both not to speak of the affair to anyone, he turned upon his heel and strode back to the curricle.

Isabella stood rooted for a moment longer, then she pulled herself together and told the driver: "The Green Dragon." She stepped into the chaise beside Bianca, who had now lapsed into further steady tears —to postpone a second, sisterly interrogation, she suspected. But she knew that whether her present distress was feigned or not, it would be pointless to question her until the storm had subsided; so she leaned back with an uncharacteristic disregard for the grubby upholstery, and turned her thoughts to what they should say to their papa.

When they came to the turnpike again she cast Zachary a repressive stare. However, that served merely to whet his curiosity, and to gossip to the postboys for rather longer than he would otherwise have done.

"Bianca, we must talk," she said, as soon as they were in motion again. "Lord, you're a sorry sight!" she went on, noting the blotched cheeks and swollen eyes under straggly curls. "Where's your bonnet? You did *have* one, I suppose?"

"Here . . ." Bianca sullenly kicked the beaver hat across the floor of the chaise with her sound foot, where her sister retrieved it and surveyed the ruined feathers. "Oh, really!" she sighed. Somehow it seemed the last straw.

"I had the headache, so I had to take it off," was the truculent reply to that. "And now my *foot* is what hurts!" She then returned to her familiar refrain of the day: "Bella, *what am I going to do?*"

"Nothing—nothing at all! I hope you have gone your length for the time being!"

Isabella was furious with her for involving them so stupidly and disastrously with their friends and neighbours. But at the same time she knew how well-intentioned she had been and, as she was clearly at the end of her tether now, she refrained from further criticisms. "Listen to me, *please*. I think it may be a stroke of good fortune that you injured your ankle." This seemingly callous remark had the desired effect: Bianca stopped snivelling at once and glared at her. "Just consider—we must face papa very soon with some explanation." She told her of the note which she had despatched home from the inn. "Now, he is bound to think it the oddest thing I didn't simply scribble him a note *before* we left to visit Polly, so if we have to return due to your damaged ankle, it will perhaps create enough of a diversion to make him forget that curious missive. We will have to say that Dandy threw you."

But this last drew a sharp protest from the sufferer. "No, I won't have poor Dandy blamed!"

"Well then, you must say you fell from him. It is only fair, after all, that you shoulder some blame for this piece of work, and I tell you frankly, if that is to be all I should count myself exceedingly fortunate, if I stood in your shoes."

"If you stood in my shoes you would be in too much agony to count yourself anything of the sort!" Bianca retorted with a surprising show of spirit, which brought a smile to her sister's lips despite her wish to be severe.

She said relentingly: "Never mind, love, we'll have

your ankle strapped up when we get to the inn. Then you can be lifted on to Dandy and we'll be home in a trice."

But this prospect only brought forth a groan from Bianca. "Papa will never believe we were going to see Polly. We've never done such a thing before."

"Ah, but we haven't had a nephew before, have we?"

Bianca was unconvinced. "It won't fadge. Gordon's disappearance is sure to come to his ears sooner or later. You heard what Sir Ranulf said—he will *call upon us . . .*"

Isabella had been deliberating on this likelihood herself. "Yes, I believe he may, and it occurs to me that the only way to prevent papa flying into a miff as soon as a Thrinby sets foot on his land is to say that we are deeply indebted to Sir Ranulf—for coming to your assistance when you took your fall."

Bianca made a wry face. "Presenting Sir Ranulf as a good Samaritan?"

"Well, he was earlier, was he not?—giving you the use of his chaise."

"Yes, but Bella, he is still certain to mention Gordon's absence to papa when he calls . . ."

"I don't believe he will," Isabella pondered. "Remember, he desired us most particularly not to speak of this to a soul—and I beg you will not," she interpolated hastily. "Did any of the servants espy you with this boy?"

"No, I was very careful—for what use it all was!" She paused a moment and then continued with a fresh surge of anxiety: "What if he doesn't find Gordon, and *then* he calls upon us? Oh, I do hope he *does* find him . . . No! What am I saying? That poor child . . . Oh, I don't understand anything anymore." She drew a grimy-looking gloved hand across her brow. "Why *did* Sir Ranulf surrender this chaise to assist our escape? He *saw* the boy—spoke to him, even. Surely he must know his own child?"

"His child?" said Isabella, startled.

"Well, one knows it must be. Illegitimate, of course," Bianca told her in worldly tones. "And now he hates the boy. Yes," she added, warming to this theme, "perhaps he is going to marry—someone else, of course, in the usual style of such men—and now he wants Gordon out of the way."

"You have been reading too many novels. He seemed very anxious indeed to find the boy, I thought."

"Well, he would be, wouldn't he?" Bianca retorted, impatient with this sad denseness from dear Bella. "You see, he would scarcely want the Family Shame running loose about the countryside."

Isabella laughed out loud for the first time in that eventful day. "Really, darling! Family shame, indeed! Explain, then, why *did* he help you both to escape from the inn?"

Bianca drew her dark brows together in a severe frown. "I don't know that yet . . . yes I do! He has only just returned home, hasn't he? Well, then, whilst he was away, his mistress—being cut off without a shilling—sent the boy to Thrinby Hall to claim his rightful inheritance."

"But why, after all these years?" Isabella said drily. "However, just supposing you are right, Sir

Ranulf must at least stand innocent of the charge of ill-treating the child, must he not?"

"Yes," admitted Bianca, with obvious reluctance. "But old Lady Thrinby would scarcely welcome an illegitimate grandson being thrust into her house, and would doubtless turn a blind eye to the servants maltreating him. Perhaps she *wanted* him to run away before her son returned!" she concluded triumphantly.

"I really don't think that is likely, you know." Although there was really no reason why Sir Ranulf shouldn't have a son, Isabella supposed; and even less reason why it should concern her if he had.

"Listen, I'm sure I am in the right of it," said her ingenious-minded sister. "The child did not own to any other name than Gordon, and he said that he had no father and *no mother anymore*. So his mother has most probably just died, and on her death-bed it would be natural that she would give solemn instructions for her son to be sent to Thrinby Hall." As Isabella still looked a trifle sceptical, Bianca patiently elaborated further: "Sir Ranulf might not have known of her death—or even of the boy's very existence—until he arrived home today. Imagine the shock!" she exclaimed, wide-eyed. "And then to find him gone!"

Isabella's steady disbelief wavered just a little at that point as she recalled Sir Ranulf's undeniably haggard aspect throughout the time they had been together.

"Well?" Bianca demanded. "If I am wrong—you tell me who that boy is."

"It is none of our business," Isabella told her

99

straitly instead, and as the chaise was just then turning into the yard of the Green Dragon, more pressing matters now commanded their attention.

When they were settling with the postboys Bianca counted up her guineas and handed them over to her sister, who had already alighted from the chaise to inform the startled landlord that his lady's assistance was needed yet again—this time to tend an injured traveller. Mercifully there were sufficient funds left to settle the reckoning, exorbitant though that seemed to Isabella, but Bianca said suddenly: "There's a guinea missing—I know there is!" Alarm once again swept across her pale features. "Oh . . . Gordon has it—he took it from me by a trick when we were here, and I forgot all about it when Sir Ranulf appeared."

This was disquieting news indeed, thought Isabella: this Gordon seemed to be a fendy lad at any time and, armed with that much wealth, who knew what further mischief he might fall into? However, there was no sense in their fretting over that now. "I expect he has lost it by this time," she said comfortingly; and Gordon's fate was then temporarily forgotten as Bianca made the painful descent from the chaise and into the inn, whilst their horses were saddled.

The sisters left the Green Dragon for home little more than an hour after Isabella and Sir Ranulf had set out from that hostelry on their earlier quest; nonetheless it was halfpast seven before the Priory gates were reached. Their ride had taken place largely in silence; Bianca being quite exhausted from pain and hunger, although the one was still making her indifferent to the other.

Isabella decided to go at once to the stables, to discover from Tom if her embarrassing message had arrived: and also, as was less likely, whether he knew what effect it had had upon her father. But the yard and stables were both deserted. Sighing, she said: "I fear you will have to dismount with only my assistance, love." She saw that Bianca's face had taken on a pinched aspect and that her ankle was now swollen.

"Never mind," the sufferer responded wearily, "I don't give a groat for anything now just as long as I can lie down upon my own bed."

Perceiving that she was at the end of her strength, Isabella quickly tied their horses, pausing only to remove the suspicious-looking portmanteau from Dandy's back: she hid it in a pile of straw until she could return and retrieve it.

With some difficulty the pair made their way to Bianca's chamber, hobbling up a little-used but awkward stairway, and luckily seeing no one. Once in her familiar surroundings again Bianca was quite prostrated and allowed herself to be put to bed.

"There, now . . . I will have a sustaining drink sent up, and then I must go to papa and explain," Isabella murmured, more to herself than to the poor invalid, and letting fall the draperies around the tent bed. She would also have to send for the doctor to examine Bianca, but saw no point in alarming her with that intelligence. She knew that their mother, if she were here, would have produced something from her box of specifics and known exactly how to go on; but both she and the box were at Hippolita's. However,

101

she remembered suddenly, cook was quite skilful with the herbs and would probably be able to recommend a remedy if applied to. She would go to her now.

The house seemed quieter and more sepulchral than usual, with the evening sun slanting dustily through the big stained-glass windows; but then it would be so, she reflected tiredly, with both mama and their brother away.

Mrs Woodley had been sitting on a stool by the hearth milling some cream, and she stood up in a startled fashion when Isabella walked into her kitchen. "Oh, Miss Isabella, there you are! And how is the poor man now? Have they got him out yet? I've had a posset ready for him this past hour or more but no one has been in for it. Oh, I hope that doesn't mean the worst . . ."

Seven

Isabella, already full of apprehension over the Banbury tale she proposed to tell her father, could only stare at Mrs Woodley, in what she realised must be a very stupid fashion. The servant's agitated greeting made no sense to her at all: but then her breath was stopped by the thought that some disaster had befallen papa whilst they had been away. Already seized with guilt, she felt this to be a judgement upon her.

"I'm s-sorry, Mrs Woodley," she stammered, "but I have this minute returned home, and have seen no one. Is it—is it my father you were speaking of?"

"Sir John? Bless you, no, miss—not that what the poor master isn't mightily distressed and blames hisself—but there, accidents will happen, won't they . . ."

"Then *who* is it, and *what* has happened?"

"That nice Mr Bradbury. Not as I had many dealings with the gentleman, of course, though he's worked for the master as long as I have. And I've never heard Woodley say a word against him in all that time, and that says a lot, miss, that does."

"You speak as if Mr Bradbury were dead!"

"And well he might be by this time . . ." Mrs Woodley put the dish of cream reverently on the table as if it contained his ashes. "As I say, I've had a posset ready since an hour back, and he was buried before then."

"*Buried*!" Isabella's mind had been running upon another riding mishap of some sort, perhaps, and now she was aghast.

"Buried right enough, in that cave thing they're digging out by the river—I never can call to mind the fancy name for it."

"The Grotto?"

"Ay," Mrs Woodley acknowledged indifferently. "Well, t'roof fell in two hours ago."

"Oh no! Is anyone else hurt?"

"Can't rightly say, miss," was the huffy response. "I shouldn't have known owt about any of it if it hadn't happened right on dinner time, and Mr Staithes looked in to tell me the master wouldn't be in yet awhile. Dinner's ruined, I may say," she concluded reproachfully.

Upon hearing this, Isabella's own predicament rushed back upon her. "I'm so sorry—that was in part my fault, but you see my sister has sustained a slight accident too. We were riding, and she had a fall and injured her ankle. Only a sprain, I think, but very painful."

"Oh, the poor lass!" cried Mrs Woodley, her maternal instincts now thoroughly diverted from the more robust Mr Bradbury. "Arnica—that's what's needed in a case like this."

"I knew I could rely on you," Isabella said gratefully. "Would it be asking too much of you to go up

104

to attend her yourself—and perhaps take her one of your sustaining drinks? It sounds to me that a doctor will have been called to the house already, but he may first be required for more serious things than a sprained ankle. Well, I must seek out papa at once and find out what is happening. He is still at the Grotto, I collect?"

"Bless you, miss, the master was doing best part of the digging, so I heard it. He thought the world of Mr Bradbury," she declared, reverting to her original mournful manner, but then continuing in brisker tones: "You leave Miss Bianca to me. I'll have her comfortable in no time at all. Now I think on—she might as well have this posset . . ." Clearly Mr Bradbury was now only of secondary importance to her.

Before she left the kitchen Isabella remembered the matter of her note: she had to know if her father had received it, before she saw him and concocted her *suggestio falsi.* "Mrs Woodley, I don't suppose you happen to know if a note was brought to the house late this afternoon?"

This query elicited quite a dramatic response, for the cook's pudgy hand flew at once to her mouth. "What a blessing you spoke of it, Miss Isabella! With all these goings on it quite slipped my mind . . . you see, young Tom brought it in from the stables." She then coughed a little over that admission. "He has a drink in the kitchen now and then, when he's not too busy like, you see, miss . . ." What Mrs Woodley chose not to reveal was that the drink was very precious tea.

"Yes, yes," said Isabella, conscious but also careless
105

of these guilty misgivings, and impatient to know the fate of her note.

"Well, I know I should've gave it to Mr Staithes, but what with him telling me that news and all, he threw me into a right state." She fished in her capacious apron pocket. "Could I ask you to bear it to Sir John, miss? I know it's not proper but—"

"Of course I will." Isabella took the note with a faint smile of irony—and with an enormous sense of relief; now she might not have to tell papa anything of the day's shocking events, save only that Bianca had suffered a fall.

"Oh, thank you, miss! I know I should've passed it on, but you see all the menfolk are out there digging: Tom went too, after his tea—" The cook's face flamed, and she looked hastily away from her young mistress.

"Don't distress yourself, I beg you," Isabella told her with quiet amusement. "I quite understand—as to the message. Oh, by the by, I should be grateful if you would try not to tax Miss Bianca with questions about her tumble: she is still very distressed, and liable to go off into tears at the very mention of it."

"As if I would, miss! I reckon I know Miss Bianca's little ways after all these years."

"Of course you do." Isabella left her on this placatory note and went with all despatch to the scene of the accident.

As she approached the river she was easily able to pick out her father's figure in his ancient tailcoat, reserved for his outdoor activities, which had once been buff-coloured and was now inclined to be of variegated hue with a multitude of dirty streaks and stains. Stepping over the flat stones across the water, she observed that the disaster had taken its toll of that durable garment: both sleeves appeared to be torn asunder at the shoulders, and had she not known of his particular attachment to the coat she would have thought this must surely be its last public appearance.

She had leisure to remark this incidental damage as her father had his back towards her, studying the chaotic scene before him: various men, including some of the house servants, were clambering about the mountain of rock and earth which almost blocked what had been a sizable cave.

"Papa," she said in an anxious and rather breathless voice as she reached his side. His eyes—apparently glazed with grief—continued to stare blankly in front of him.

In some suspense—for she could not see Mr Bradbury's familiar features anywhere—she repeated, more strongly: "Papa?" and tugged at one of the ravaged sleeves.

"Mm? Oh, Isabella, my dear child," he said in lacklustre fashion. "The tragedy of it, eh?—just look . . ." He flung out an arm dramatically.

She looked again as he bade her, but could discern little beyond the obvious enough fact of the unnatural upheaval. "Papa—Mr Bradbury—is he still beneath all that?" she asked, appalled.

"Bradbury?" he repeated in seeming surprise. "No, Bradbury's in fine fettle: we had him out of there in a trice, none the worse for it—bar a bit of a shake-up, of course. I've sent him off to put some timber felling in hand."

His daughter now shot him a startled glance. *"Timber felling,* papa?" It hardly seemed a fitting occupation for someone who had just been buried alive.

"Yes, you see we must have something to support the roof—what's left of it," Sir John replied abstractedly. "It's terrible, *terrible,* and I had been hoping to start mounting the shells in only another day or two," he declared with angry bitterness.

The situation brought home to Isabella just how obsessed her father was with his endless schemes for the Priory. "Was poor Mr Bradbury covered over for long?" she asked him with a shudder.

But Sir John treated that inquiry too as a distraction from more important matters. "Pooh, only fifteen minutes: or I suppose it might have been a half-hour. But the fellow wasn't buried precisely, merely *walled in,* you might say. He could stand up straight enough the whole time."

Isabella wondered how long half an hour could seem, when you were walled up in the dark and expecting the next roof fall at any moment; but her father, who conspicuously lacked this kind of imaginative capacity, had returned to his prior concern.

"You see, Bella, I'd conjured up a vision of how it should all be when your mama returns home: with those magnificent iridescent shells lining the walls—and of course the ceiling as well. Just picture the effect of the mass glister by candlelight . . . Ah well, I suppose we shall reach that high point one day."

"By candlelight!" exclaimed Isabella, fearful that One-eyed Jack really was destined to take up permanent residence in the Grotto for the purpose of being a special human effect in the scheme.

"Yes: I thought the candelabra from the Little Armoury might suit—what say you? Placed upon the refectory table from the Small Dining Hall."

His daughter, calling to mind that that item of furniture measured at least fifteen feet, said in bewilderment: "A table of *that* size, papa?" Although in truth she really wished to know, why a table of any size in a mere cave?

"Well, you can't sit less than twenty to be a regular dinner party, now can you, my dear?" he responded, evidently rather puzzled by her lack of perspicacity. "It would have been such a fine surprise for your mama. She could have entertained a few discerning friends to a dinner of a sort they'd never experienced before in their lives: positively sublime, if one could count upon a full moon lighting the river scene outside. But when will that be now?" He heaved a deep sigh of frustration and regret.

Isabella could well believe that the Grotto dinner would have come as a surprise to those friends he had in mind; whether it would have surprised her mother she rather doubted, after all these years of ruthless transformation. At some stage in the past it had become tacitly understood that Sir John's 'improvements' should henceforth be applied to the grounds, and that the house itself should suffer no more battlemented wings or tracery windows. However, she had never heard her mama utter any real complaint against the gloomy pile they lived in, although from time to time she would refurbish a room to her own more conventional taste.

"I do see it has been a cruel disappointment—such a truly delightful notion," she said tactfully. "I know

109

it cannot possibly match your own conception, papa, but how would it be if we were to have an ordinary moonlight picnic instead? I remember how we all loved them as children."

He smiled at her with affection, but then shook his still fine head and gave another sigh. "As you say, it would scarcely be the same . . . Oh, what a vexatious business it is to have a scheme in one's head and be unable to—" He waved an arm violently at the mud and rubble.

"Won't you now come in for dinner, papa? It is very late."

"Good God, is it? Yes, I suppose it must be. You have partaken of yours, I collect?"

She seized upon the opening thus afforded her. "Well, no, as a matter of fact we have had our own mishaps today too." She told him that Bianca had taken a fall while out riding.

"Dear me, poor child! Not badly hurt, eh? But you should have told me sooner, not let me ramble on like this." Bianca had always been his favourite daughter.

"No, just a sprain, although do you not think Doctor James should take a look at it to be certain?"

"Indeed he must." And Tom from the stables, who had rather enjoyed the excitement of helping to dig out the overseer, was now plucked from the debris of the cave and sent post-haste to summon the family physician. Sir John then abandoned the site of his latest plaything and stiffly accompanied Isabella back to the house.

"I do not know how I should have gone on," she told him as they walked, "had it not been for a neighbour's timely assistance—he was everything helpful."

110

"And who was that, pray? It was very kind in him, and I must make a point of conveying my thanks."

She gave a nervous little laugh. "Well, I didn't recognize him at first, of course, but it seems it was— Sir Ranulf."

He stopped his pace abruptly. "*What*? That fellow? Whyever did he have to interfere? We stand in no need of help from that quarter . . ."

"But *I* was grateful, papa!" she protested, with a heat that surprised herself. "He—he impressed me as being very proper both in manner and address," she added more diffidently.

"So I should hope, by God . . ."

Isabella did not feel inclined to break the ensuing heavy silence, but then her parent declared somewhat ponderously: "However, the charge shall not be levelled at *me* that *I* do not know how to respond in a correct and punctilious fashion: I will send a note of thanks." He paused, clearly very struck by this act of self-sacrifice.

"I don't think that will be at all necessary," Isabella said hastily. "Sir Ranulf was riding out from the Hall at the time—I doubt he would be there to receive any thanks."

Sir John looked relieved. "Didn't know the fellow had returned, even. Of course I take no interest in their doings. He seems to be a here-and-thereian all the time—but then that's only what one would expect from that man's son . . . Very well, if you think it is needless, I will allow myself to be persuaded."

Isabella breathed a sigh of relief as this first fence was successfully cleared; although she was only too

111

aware that the matter of the missing boy was by no means disposed of.

*   *   *

Whilst Sir John de Hyville and Isabella were sitting down to their belated dinner, not a mile away from them Lady Thrinby and her daughter were just rising from a similarly delayed repast after suffering a day of equal disorder.

Her ladyship and Laetitia walked to the drawing-room, leaving Arthur to his solitary port. Her son-in-law, reflected her ladyship, must surely be the only gentleman in existence who brought a book into dinner with him to read when the cloth was removed. That habit of his was not confined to such times as now, when it might be deemed forgivable though outlandish, but on one occasion—and one only—her late husband had reproved him for this same lapse before company.

"I still think we should have dined at the customary hour, mama," Laetitia was complaining as they took up their places. Lady Thrinby had gone to a comfortable Jacobean chair, positioned for her carefully by the butler in the direct rays of the evening sun. Laetitia chose a straight chair in a corner, quite dark by contrast in the large room.

"I know you do, dear," her ladyship said equably, "but we were not to know when Ranulf would return, and I did wish him to join us on his first night home, if that were possible."

"I am well aware of the reason," Laetitia retorted in her tones of constant peevishness. "*I* have to think of Arthur first. If Arthur eats only a *minute* after

112

seven, he suffers from dreadful spasms of dyspepsia in the early hours: then neither of us is able to snatch a wink of sleep thereafter. Have you any rhubarb in the house?—and perhaps I should have another bed made up in my old room . . ."

"The rhubarb I will certainly have made up for you: the bed I will not. In my view a wife's place is by her husband's side if he is indisposed, not sleeping comfortably at the other end of the house," Lady Thrinby averred with a certain satisfaction. She wondered in passing how Arthur was able to endure their invariably lengthy visits to their more fashionable relatives, who would not sit down to dinner before eight.

Her rebuke was met with a sulky silence for a moment, but Laetitia soon rallied. "I cannot understand how you can tolerate to sit in the sun like that, mama. Why, just a touch of those harmful rays would bring a migraine upon me for weeks."

"You must allow me to know my own preferences and capabilities after nigh on seventy years—and yours likewise, I may say."

She turned a little to regard her daughter, but could only discern a shadowy outline in the gloomy depths of the apartment: the dissatisfied dark eyes and petulant line of the mouth she did not need to see, however. "You were never used to suffer the migraine." (Although, her ladyship chuckled to herself, a decade spent with Arthur Beckforth would be likely to set up a permanent headache in anyone.)

"Nor do I now—unless I foolishly expose myself to the sun!"

But this observation brought such a dark look to her mother's features that Laetitia deemed it wise to

113

change the direction of her criticism. "I trust, in any event, that this room is kept shaded in the afternoon to protect the furniture and this carpet—which I have always considered to be a particularly fine one." In fact, her brother had once said that the carpet's garish colours ruined the drawing-room; which had naturally caused Laetitia to admire it from that day.

Lady Thrinby did not rise to this fresh bait; she was well used to her disputatious and unuaseful nature, and did not permit it to ruffle her unduly. She had rather Laetitia exercised her spite upon her than direct it against Ranulf, who was inclined to flare up against his silly sister. That she was destined to suffer a good deal of such harassment in the ensuing days was only too plain to her—even without her daughter's next remark.

"I cannot for the life of me imagine why you permitted Ranulf to foist this child upon you in the first place—just look at the trouble it has caused! Unless, of course," she added pointedly, "there is some particular reason why you should have agreed to do so."

"And *I* cannot imagine what you mean me to infer from that innuendo," Lady Thrinby said with another quelling glare. But now Laetitia had the bit between her teeth.

"Of course you do, mama! And so I can only suppose that you know who this unspeakable boy is!"

"I will not have you refer to him in that derogatory manner. He is a perfectly ordinary child, full of *joie de vivre* and animal spirits quite natural to his years. That he should prove too much of a handful for little Miss What's-her-name surprises me not at all. He reminds me so very much of Ranulf at the same age."

Now that, her ladyship thought to herself, was a remark of extraordinary silliness in the circumstances: she must be getting senile. "No, I do not know the precise parentage of Gordon," she went on before Laetitia could make the inevitable comment, "but I trust Ranulf implicitly. If he believes it necessary and fitting that this boy should stay here—for a very limited time, I may say—then I am happy to oblige him *without* harbouring any unpleasant suspicions on the matter."

This speech merely fuelled Laetitia's permanent resentment against her brother: he had always been the favourite, and this latest outrage proved beyond doubt to her what a blinkered view her mother took, and had aways taken, of his every action.

The drawing-room door now opened to admit Arthur, who shuffled towards a seat by his mother-in-law; not, as she knew very well, in order to engage her in polite conversation for the rest of the evening, but just because that was the best place near the light for him to read. His tall lean frame, taller and leaner than usual in the unrelieved black of his evening dress, buckled awkwardly into the low chair. After a cursory nod at them both he opened his book and rested it on his bony satin-clad knees.

Lady Thrinby saw without surprise that he had a bound copy of *The Gentleman's Magazine*, taken from her late husband's library. Too mean to subscribe to it himself, invariably when staying at Thrinby Hall he immersed himself in its erudite pages, the better to bore his fellows with learned expositions upon the latest improvements in the construction of mill wheels or plough shares, or a new-invented stove chimney: his memory for such detail was prodigious. This meant that whilst his wife gave their successive hostesses the benefit of her firm advice upon the running of their households, Arthur would undertake to instruct their menfolk in the management of their estates. As far as Lady Thrinby was concerned, her son-in-law's sole redeeming feature was his taciturnity in female company—which was clearly held to be beneath his notice.

Once again she gave silent thanks that this doleful pair had not, for whatever reasons, presented her with grandchildren. For years she had awaited with apprehension the arrival of a brood of little Beckforths but now felt confident that this was not to be. However, that did not mean she was averse to becoming a grandmother before she died, and, with that partly in mind, she had tried to turn Ranulf's thoughts in the positive direction of matrimony this last season. She wondered if she had been successful . . .

"It was in '08 that Ranulf fell in with that ramshackle set, of course," Laetitia was now saying. "So-called friends from Cambridge, I collect." She paused in this new assault to help herself to three macaroons from the plate held out to her by a footman, who, with the butler, had just brought in the tea tray. "*Arthur*!—you had best not touch these tonight!"

Her husband paid not the least regard to those words; and her mother would have been sensible to ignore the former remark—and would have done, had she not been lost in her own thoughts. As it was she said vaguely: " '08, dear? Why, that's an age ago. What has that to say to anything?"

116

"I would have thought that to be quite obvious in the circumstances! The sudden appearance of a seven year old harvest, sown from wild oats at the time I spoke of . . . I choose not to be more specific, mama."

Lady Thrinby was doubly incensed: that Letty should voice such scurrilous things was bad enough, but to do so in front of Ranulf's own servants was intolerable. "You talk in riddles, I fear, and you know I never could make much sense of them," she said harshly, and turned at once to the butler. "Headcorn, would you see to it that a very large draught of rhubarb is prepared and sent up to the visitors' apartment?"

When the two servants had withdrawn, Laetitia, unable to resist the slightest opportunity for criticism, said: "Mama, I did not know where to look! There was no call to request poor Arthur's rhubarb quite so publicly."

This final goad decided her ladyship to administer a severe set-down to her daughter. "*Your* recent conversation, my girl, discovers neither good sense nor good manners," she began trenchantly.

Thoroughly irritated and distressed by Ranulf's continued absence and the boy's disappearance, she now came within a whisker of turning her daughter out of the house there and then; knowing full well that whatever she said to her Laetitia was incapable of letting the subject of Ranulf and the child rest now. However, she concluded in dangerous rising tones: "—As to your brother, I do not wish to hear another word of your vulgar aspersions upon him as long as you are under his roof and receiving his hospitality."

At that point, Arthur, who had remained uniquely oblivious of this family discord all about him, looked up at the word hospitality, picked up his cup, gazed myopically at his white-faced spouse, and enquired of neither of them in particular: "Is there more tea, do you suppose?—and another macaroon would be most acceptable . . ."

Eight

One glance at his youngest child, her face almost as pale as the fine lawn pillow which framed it, was enough to make Sir John contemplate writing to Malvina urging her return: then, when Bianca opened her eyes and seemed to eye him almost fearfully, whimpering in a piteous fashion in response to his kindest inquiries, he knew that it was imperative to send for her mother.

With an eloquent glance at Isabella, who stood watchfully at the foot of the pretty silk tent bed (their mother had kept all trace of Gothic fantasy from the girls' bedchambers), Sir John turned upon his heel and quit the room. Isabella hurried after him, pausing to lay a hand on Bianca's shoulder as she left her. "Don't fret, love: all will be well."

Her father was standing gloomily in the outside passage. "The child has suffered more than a sprained ankle, I'll be bound!" he said in a voice bordering on the accusatory. "Are you sure she wasn't kicked?"

"Yes, papa, quite sure, and Mrs Woodley confirms that it is no more than a nasty twist."

"Humph. I do not scruple to say I shall set more

store by the leech's opinion that the cook's. Where *is* the man?" He drew out his watch in an agitated manner. "I will be in the bookroom if you want me—writing to your mama." He strode off towards the stairs.

"Pray don't alarm her without cause!" Isabella called after him as she followed. "Would it not be better to wait for Doctor James's verdict?" She was presently torn between wishing for her mother to return and take charge of the household, and dreading the complications which might ensue in that quarter when Sir Ranulf paid his threatened visit. But it was clear she now had no say in the matter: Sir John had quite resolved to recall his lady.

"That Thrinby fellow—is he at the root of all this pother?" Sir John demanded, causing a further tremor of apprehension to run through her. "If he did or said *anything* untoward to that innocent child, I'll run him to ground if he's sailing the China Sea!" he declared confusedly.

"Papa, I give my solemn word that Sir Ranulf behaved impeccably and rendered us invaluable assistance."

"Humph," he grunted again, in a way that was still most sceptical.

"You know how easy it is to overset Bianca's nerves. She has suffered a bad shaking, but after a good night's rest she will be as right as a trivet. I'm sure Doctor James will bear me out," she said confidently as they walked downstairs and past the grandfather clock in the hall: she noted that its mailed fists now stood at a few seconds to nine o'clock. It felt to her like a lifetime, not a mere five hours, since she

120

had last consulted it before setting out to look for her sister.

"I only hope you may be in the right of it," Sir John replied, disappearing into the bookroom, and his dejected hollow tones seemed to be echoed by the sepulchral chiming of the hour at that moment.

Isabella was right: Doctor James was a robust member of the faculty who did not pay much heed to female languishing. He merely examined the ankle— in the process destroying Mrs Woodley's excellent binding—and replaced it with a bandage that was too tight. Observing his patient's acute reaction to this procedure, he took her pulse, expecting to find it tumultuous: as indeed it was. Satisfied that all was as it should be, he recommended in his profound professional manner a sleeping draught and complete rest, and then departed to reassure Sir John. Which, Isabella reflected later, had been by far his most useful function; for she threw away the noxious draught, untied the bandage, and sent for the cook to replace both.

Under Isabella's and Mrs Woodley's more tender care, Bianca revived quite well and when, two days later, Lady Malvina arrived home, the patient was altogether more tranquil than anyone had expected. For both sisters the bizarre events of their afternoon with Sir Ranulf gradually faded, and seemed almost dreamlike by contrast with their mother's news of Hippolita and the baby. The matter of the runaway boy began to recede from their minds; though not entirely. And after a fourth day of total silence from Thrinby Hall, Bianca said when they were alone together: "Bella, you will ride into the village again today, will you not? Someone *must* know if Sir Ranulf is back: though if anything dreadful had happened to Gordon, surely we would have heard of it by now?"

Isabella felt she was placed in a difficult position. It was true they had many friends in the neighbourhood, scattered over the sparsely populated parish, but it would look very odd in her if she began to make daily calls upon them; and more particularly if she also started to display a sudden interest in the Thrinby family. The coldness between the Priory and Thrinby Hall was well-known.

Consequently, before deciding how best to set about her search for information—and she was still in lively dread of coming face to face with Sir Ranulf the minute she ventured past their own gates—she rode towards the belvedere. She had decided to scale its heights once more and survey the Thrinby grounds; although not without a twinge of guilt, for she could not help but think of it as a 'damnable spy tower' after Sir Ranulf's biting remarks. She had to place both hands on the great iron ring to turn it and open the door, and as she did so she heard a sound which at first she dismissed as a particularly agonising screak of the giant hinges.

However, the noise came again when the door was still, and, convinced she was hearing those same chilling screams from Thrinby Hall as before, she ran up the stairs at once.

But—just as before—there was nothing to be seen stirring below in their neighbour's park. Disconsolate, and not a little shaken, she quit the tower and rode slowly back to the house, feeling quite unable to pursue her inquiries beyond their own boundary that day.

She had not meant to mention this disturbing incident to Bianca, fearing that it might shatter what peace of mind she had managed to regain over the past few days; but when the pair of them had a long prose together that evening, she decided to risk touching upon the subject of the Thrinby screams.

"Did you ever discover from the boy what they might be?"

Bianca did not answer that question, but shook her head in a way that seemed somehow evasive.

Isabella shrugged. "Well, whatever they are, they are still to be heard."

To her astonishment, those few and faintly ominous words made her sister's face light up. "Are they the same—the *very* same cries we heard that first time, Bella?" she asked breathlessly. "Why, that's *Gordon*! Oh, then they must have found him!" And if she had not been confined to her chair she looked as if she might have executed a joyful dance at that point.

"You mean the *boy* makes that hideous noise?"

Bianca wrinkled her nose. "Yes, all the time—it's ghastly beyond anything."

"I know it is! But why didn't you tell me this?"

"I—well, I'm not sure." Bianca was now a little shamefaced. "I suppose I wanted you to go on believing in the dreadful happenings there. In some sort it seemed to help to justify my taking Gordon away."

"Are you saying that you no longer consider he *was* ill-treated?" Isabella, who had never seen the boy, and who still wanted to be scrupulously fair to

Bianca, had nonetheless entertained grave doubts on that head ever since her own meeting with Sir Ranulf and hearing his indignant sarcasm on the subject of any ill-treatment.

Bianca was silent a moment, pleating the hailstone muslin of her skirt between nervous fingers. "I suppose he might have been . . . exaggerating a trifle, the way Julia says small boys do," she admitted in a low voice. Then, in a sudden outburst, she cried: "I have been utterly idiotic, haven't I?"

"No, not idiotic, love—perhaps naïve, but then you have no small brothers."

"Nor have you, but you wouldn't have done anything so downright fat-witted, would you?" Bianca declared bitterly. "*Why* can't I *ever* act in a proper fashion like everyone else? Lord, I cannot imagine what Mr Amersham will think of me when Julia tells him . . ."

"Oh, don't take it to heart so! I blame myself a good deal for filling your head with high-flown notions the day before, about helping people. Still, if the boy is safely back there is no real harm done—except for that, of course." She indicated Bianca's ankle resting on the footstool.

"Due retribution," Bianca said in a doom-laden voice, and surveying her foot so lugubriously that her sister could not stifle a gurgle of laughter.

"I'm sorry, love," she amended at once. "I know it's not in the least amusing for you to be confined to the house in this sad way. But never mind, now that the boy is restored you will be able to look forward to going to see Polly and our new nephew, as soon as you can walk again."

"Sir Ranulf might descend upon us at any time," said the invalid, refusing to be cheered.

"Well, at least it does not appear likely that he intends to have you transported, or cast into Newgate for kidnapping!"

"Don't forget papa's wrath, though, if *he* should find out," Bianca murmured, evidently looking upon that as a third alternative of almost equal direness.

"If you regard my opinion, I don't believe we shall see Sir Ranulf after this interval. I'd hazard he will not have the smallest desire to meet either of us again." And as she said that, Isabella felt a sudden paradoxical disappointment that he had not called upon them.

When a week had elapsed since that fateful day, even Bianca was inclined to think that Isabella must be right in her surmise; her spirits had recovered their tone by then and her foot was much less painful.

One afternoon the two sisters took advantage of a fine interlude after several dull and uninviting days, and sallied forth into the gardens. Bianca was still unable to walk any distance but attained the rose garden without much difficulty. She sat in the shady arbour while Isabella gathered some of their late-blooming northern roses.

"We are fortunate in being home in time to see papa's new *Cuisse de Nymphe*. What a beautiful shade—and this is the first year it has given such a magnificent display."

"Yes: but what a shocking name! Papa's Nymph's Thigh!" Bianca giggled, taking some blooms and sniffing them appreciatively.

But the distant sound of an approaching carriage

turned this pleasure to dismay, and the two exchanged alarmed glances. "Go and see who it is, *please*!" begged Bianca, "for I cannot. But pray keep out of sight, in case—!"

Obediently Isabella stole along to a vantage point where she could overlook the drive—albeit not very clearly through the mass of foliage which clothed their ground in the summer months. However, that it was a very dashing curricle and pair driven by a gentleman was clear enough, and the sun glinting on the bright paintwork suggested it might be a brand new vehicle: beyond that she could discover nothing, and the visitor soon disappeared from her sight as he approached the curve to the main entrance.

Upon hearing this, Bianca was sure of the worst. Gentlemen driving elegant new carriages were seldom, if ever, seen at the Priory, and their neighbour was the only person likely to be presenting himself in this way. For a moment she cherished the fond hope that it was Mr Carleton Amersham come to call, but then had to admit that it was in the highest degree unlikely. "Well, whoever it is, they must seek us out," she declared cravenly.

Isabella was not convinced that this was their best course: she had a dreadful vision of Sir Ranulf being received by their mama with a forced civility which would dwindle rapidly into gelid hauteur if even a hint of criticism of her daughters should pass the visitor's lips. "No, I think I at least should go up to the house," she said with reluctance.

She did not hurry, and was just in time to see the gentleman walking round to the front of the house from the direction of the stables; the dazzling carriage was nowhere in sight.

"*John!*" she cried. "Is it really you?"

"Hello, Bella!—of course it's me! Dash it, you look as though you've just seen one of father's headless ghosts stalking the battlements!"

Brother and sister were facing each other now. Isabella was struck, as she always was after an absence these days, by his handsome and impressive looks, so much like his father's; although in the ordinary way she did think his lack of interest in fashionable dress a pity—but not today. Beneath the long silk-lined driving-coat he wore immaculate cream leather breeches and a spotted cravat, none of which she had seen before, and he carried obviously new York tan gloves.

"I saw the strange carriage, and now *you* in all this unaccustomed splendour—is it any wonder I am surprised?" she said with affectionate raillery. "Besides, we were not in expectation of your coming."

"I know, but I couldn't keep away from the bosom of my family a moment longer," he said in mock-serious tones, then added with genuine eagerness: "So you saw the curricle, eh? Isn't it bang up?"

She laughed. "So that's why you've come home—to shine us all down and cut a dash in the neighbourhood."

"You wrong me—you know that is not my style. Though mind you," he added, a glint in his eye, "I think I *did* make quite an impression upon the lady who inquired of me the way to Thrinby Hall."

"The Hall!"

"There's no need to look as sick as a cushion! I

merely gave her directions on the road—even father would permit one that much licence with our neighbours' affairs, I fancy. Look, where is everybody? Delightful though this chit-chat is I have no wish to stand here all afternoon."

"Papa is somewhere in the gardens about his Improvements, as you would imagine. Mama is in the house—but first come and see Bianca." She thought this might afford her a good opportunity to tell John in private about their unfortunate entanglement with the Thrinby family, in the hope that he might be able to help in some way if the need arose. "I left her sitting in the arbour."

John thereupon put in a cavil about being too tired after driving the length and breadth of England to tramp so far to see a lively young miss, and why couldn't she come and see him?

"She cannot—well, not very easily—she has hurt her ankle, you see."

Isabella walked him slowly back to the arbour, telling him the whole sorry tale. "What a dashed cork-brained thing to do!" was his immediate brotherly comment, then he opined in similar vein: "Only Bianca could fall into a scrape like that! You're sure this wretched lad is found now, are you?"

"Almost sure. He screeches like a parrot in the most unmistakable way, and that sound has again been heard in the land since then."

As they approached the rose arbour, unseen, John suddenly gave a wicked grin and put his finger to his lips. He began intoning: "Oh yes indeed, ma'am, it's a *very* serious felony, kidnapping is . . .!" Isabella made a furious face at him when she understood his

128

intention, but he continued blithely: "—still, I dare-say the beak won't be too hard on the young lady if she has a pretty face, and talks to him nicely like. If you ask me, she'll get off lightly with transportation!"

Bianca had tottered to her feet—the roses thrown on the ground testifying to the haste of her action—and she faced them both with an expression every bit as stricken as a poor wretch's awaiting transporta-tion. "Pay no heed, love," Isabella said to her at once. "It is only John come home to tease you."

"Oh! You—you beast!" Bianca sank down on to the seat again, and addressed her sister in accents of hor-ror: "You haven't *told him*?"

"Yes, there is no necessity to hide the affair from John—who has never supported papa's silly feud with the Thrinbys, and who may well stand our ally, I thought, if Sir Ranulf should finally make his threat-ened call."

Bianca thought this over. "I suppose he may be useful," she conceded grudgingly. At that moment John gave a cry of pain as a thorn from one of the roses he was retrieving for her stabbed his fingers. "Serves you right," she told him with satisfaction.

"There's gratitude for you!" he grumbled, standing up with a weary stretch and handing the bouquet to Isabella. "No, I scarcely know anything of the Hall people, having at least respected father's wishes over the years. Besides, Sir Ranulf must be nigh on ten years my senior, although I've on occasion espied him at a distance at some tonnish gathering in Town. He belongs to a different set, y'know."

"I fancy he might," said Isabella drily. "Unless, of

course, he too is consumed with a holy passion to build bridges."

Before John could use this as an excuse to launch into a eulogy upon one of the two new London bridges at present under construction, which he had stayed behind after his family especially to observe, she asked him: "Who was the lady you encountered making her way to the Hall?"

"How should I know, merely after exchanging pleasantries?" he retorted.

"Perhaps a future Lady Thrinby?" Isabella suggested curiously.

"Who knows?—he's a lucky dog if that's true: a dashed handsome female, although a bit high in the instep for my taste."

"*There*!" put in Bianca, "I told you he was most likely contemplating marriage, did I not?"

"Amongst a host of other fantastic speculations, if I remember aright," Isabella rallied her; although in fact she was vastly intrigued by this mysterious lady herself.

* * *

Sir Ranulf, when Headcorn informed him that a Miss Helen Rishworth had called, and was in the Little Drawing Room, felt more staggered than intrigued.

"Is Miss Rishworth unaccompanied?" he asked the butler, in part to delay his meeting with this wholly unexpected guest, but more, to try to discover what could have brought her a distance of well over two hundred miles from her Hertfordshire home; to which place, as far as he was aware, Lord Rishworth had intended conveying her immediately after his own momentous interview with his lordship in Town.

"Yes—unless you are thinking of her maid, sir." Sensing his master's uncertainty, Headcorn cleared his throat and vouchsafed: "I did happen to observe that the lady arrived in a private chaise, and I gained an impression she had travelled some distance. Perhaps I am wrong, sir, but there did also seem to be a goodly number of bandboxes and portmanteaux handed down."

"Good God!" Sir Ranulf exclaimed involuntarily, but his mind was boggling at the implications of Miss Rishworth's presence—and if she meant to *stay* . . . !

He had told his mother of his matrimonial plans soon after he had recovered Gordon, but she was totally unacquainted with the Rishworths and her response to the proposed match had fallen short of the ecstatic. She had also been critical of his conduct in the matter, telling him frankly that she thought it odd that he had not stayed in the capital long enough to propose to the lady herself and secure an answer. This view of his actions had not occurred to him: knowing only too well that, once he was set upon a course, he had a tendency to rush his fences, he had deliberately sought to give both himself and his intended, time for reflection by quitting the scene for a space. Well, now that Miss Rishworth was only a couple of rooms away from him, and if, as seemed likely, she was paying more than a formal call, his mother would be able to judge the wisdom of his choice for herself at leisure—and so would his sister.

The latter prospect appalled him: Letty had not been told of his impending betrothal, and this omission no doubt would add to her natural spitefulness; furthermore she had excelled herself of late with constant sly hints about the boy. And what of Gordon? He had every hope that a new home and future would be arranged for him soon, but it was scarcely possible that it could be contrived in a week or two. Meanwhile, a good deal of his own time was being absorbed in exercising control of his movements so that he should not abscond again.

Headcorn waited patiently, an interested eye resting upon his master. "The lady expressed a particular wish to speak with you, sir," he murmured into the silence.

"Yes, man, yes," Sir Ranulf said edgily. "Tell me—does she appear—well, distressed or agitated in any way?"

"Indeed no, sir. I would say quite the contrary."

—So then what the devil had she come for, unannounced and uninvited? Sir Ranulf felt a most unfitting surge of annoyance at this arbitrary behaviour on the part of the lady of his choice. But there was only one way to get to the bottom of the business and so he consented to see Miss Rishworth forthwith.

When Headcorn presently regaled the other upper servants with the intelligence that Sir Ranulf had just received a most attractive lady—and with all the enthusiasm of a buckle-maker hearing that shoestrings were coming in fashion—speculation was rife amongst them.

Nine

Sir Ranulf approached the Little Drawing Room a prey to all manner of apprehensions which, as he vaguely realized, were scarcely the ones which should have been ruffling his composure at such a time. Instead of feeling overjoyed at this unexpected chance to propose to Miss Rishworth in person at last, he was simply irritated that she should have placed him in an invidious situation.

What, he wondered crossly, was Rishworth thinking of to allow his daughter to career unchaperoned about the country in this style? Could it be that his lordship had turned her out of the house after some altercation—over his own offer of marriage, perhaps? Other thoughts of an even wilder nature chased through his mind, and he arrived at the threshold of the drawing-room on Headcorn's heels in a state of considerable anxiety, thankful only that Laetitia had not intercepted him en route.

The situation was saved by the bizarre character of the Little Drawing Room (which, due to familiarity, he had almost forgotten) and by the astonishing composure of Miss Rishworth; who seemed to him to be *posée* far beyond her twenty-five years. He had been aware of this quality in her character in Town—indeed it was one of her attractions for him—but somehow on his home ground its effect was more marked. Later, he was even inclined to think that the whole of the credit for smoothing their encounter lay with her, rather than the novel surroundings in which she found herself: a lesser person might certainly have been overwhelmed by them.

"Sir Ranulf!" She advanced towards him extending her hand. Although not given to kissing ladies' hands, he had little alternative in this instance as it was clearly expected of him; and Miss Rishworth, he reminded himself once more, was not any lady but his future wife.

"Welcome to Thrinby Hall, Miss Rishworth—and to what do I owe this unexpected pleasure, may I ask?"

"Oh, *Helen*, I think in the circumstances, do you not agree?" she said, not in the arch tones which might have accompanied that suggestion but with brisk matter-of-factness.

Whilst he was murmuring polite agreement she continued: "Forgive me for divesting myself of my pelisse, but I found the heat in the carriage very oppressive, and could not wait to throw off some clothes."

Sir Ranulf eyed her cool-looking white muslin dress with some envy, and said he hoped she was tolerably comfortable now; then he offered to ring for some refreshment. That accomplished, he thought he had some hope of extracting an answer to his original question—but it was not to be.

"Pray sit down, er, Helen: though I own the furniture is not as inviting as it might be!" He gestured somewhat ruefully at the angular Egyptian sofas and stools.

But Miss Rishworth remained standing—or, more accurately, walking—while she observed: "Thank you, but I am vastly glad to stretch my legs after the hours in that cramping chaise. Indeed, I have been much restored by awaiting you in this fascinating, not to say extraordinary apartment. You know, I don't believe I have seen its equal—certainly not in the Egyptian Hall by Piccadilly. It exhibits a deep interest: quite beyond the commonplace Memphian influence which one sees everywhere one goes these days." Her perambulations had now taken her to a long low sofa whose gilded ends supported a pair of thoughtful sphinxes upon each; she patted one as if it were a live spaniel. "This, I am persuaded, bears every sign of authenticity—unlike some of the perfect *monstrosities* one sees in the Egyptian Taste." She glanced across at her silenced host. "I had no notion you were a connoisseur and collector of antiquities, but it pleases me to the quick that—"

"I can lay no claim to the credit," Sir Ranulf interposed hastily. "My father was a scholar and great traveller and he gathered together this unique collection over many years. He was a leading authority on the subject, and left behind notebooks and papers which were intended for a book—an English counterpart of Baron Denon's work." As he spoke he saw the undisguised disappointment on her face.

"So you know nothing of all this?" She waved an arm comprehensively around the lofty room with its frieze of Pharaohs and animal deities, in unfashionable colours of terra cotta, black and citrine, and the exotic if uncomfortable furnishings.

"Well, inevitably I have learned something of it, having grown up with it." Sir Ranulf, from being grateful for this diversion, which had eased the first awkwardness of their meeting, now wished to turn the conversation into more practical channels; but he found that singularly difficult to accomplish.

"Pray tell me, then, what does this curious figure here signify?" she was asking, even as he phrased a quite different question of his own. Moreover, even the mundane presence of Headcorn some minutes later with the refreshments seemed unlikely at first to direct the talk from Horus, Nekhebet and Thoth to the much more pressing matter as to why Miss Rishworth was here at all, and how long she intended to stay: as to the latter, he felt it in the highest degree improbable that his wishes were going to be consulted at all. Never had he felt so helpless, not even with his sister; where at least he was usually able to give a Roland for an Oliver. However, he did contrive (whilst his guest quenched her thirst for a moment after a long discussion upon the significance of the Ibis) to say to her rather desperately: "Miss Rishworth—Helen—you did not, I collect, travel a considerable distance merely to listen to an historical lecture which you could just as well have heard—indeed, a far superior one—at the Royal Institution?"

She smiled at him over her glass; and she had a pleasant way of using her wide blue eyes which, he remembered, had first caught his attention at the time of their first meeting at the Duchess of Cumberland's assembly. "No, of course I did not—although I fear you mistake the other matter. I, as a mere female, am not allowed within the august portals of the Institution." She paused, then went restlessly over to the table and picked up a small statue there. "Now this representation of—Sebek, did you say?—must be quite unique."

Seeing his father's most precious item, the pride of his collection, and one which family and servants alike were forbidden to touch, being handled and regarded as if it were bruised fruit at a market, at once broke the spell for Sir Ranulf and he strode across to her. "Yes, it *is* unique, quite priceless, thousands of years old, and *we do not touch it*!" He took it from her grasp and replaced it with the utmost care on the table.

"I am so sorry, do forgive me! Would it not be safer under glass?" she asked, seemingly unabashed.

"There is no call for that, we keep the doors locked at all usual times . . . Miss Rishworth," he went on in determined tones, "you were about to tell me why you are here." Those words sounded abominably brusque to his ears, and no way to welcome one's future spouse into the bosom of the family, but he felt he had been driven to it.

The blue eyes smiled at him again. "Helen, *please*! Why, I am here to see *you*, of course!" she told him disarmingly. "You did speak to my papa, did you not?"

Unnerved by this swift change of manner he said: "Yes—yes, I did."

She gave a hard little laugh. "I did not think that even he would be mistaken about such a matter!"

"—But if you had waited I had, of course, every intention of inviting both you and Lord Rishworth here to meet my mother, and everything could then have been set in hand to—"

"Oh, papa wouldn't come, you know," she cut across him abruptly. "Can't abide travelling! You can have no idea of the rubs he can cast in one's way just in returning from London into Hertfordshire."

Sir Ranulf now found himself wishing that his lordship had cast a few more such rubs in her path when this present journey was proposed. He said tentatively: "Your father was happy that you should undertake such an arduous journey alone for the purpose of calling here?"

She looked more than a little surprised at that question. "Happy? Oh, I daresay he might be, if he knew of it. I told him of my invitation from Lady Eleanor, to join her party at Scarborough. The Melgates hire a house there every year at this time and occasionally I make up their party. They always comprise the most dead-bores imaginable, but I daresay you will know the Baxters of Hambleton?"

But Sir Ranulf, having already delved exhaustively into the Egyptian dynasties, had no intention of repeating the performance with Yorkshire's illustrious families. "So you make your way to Scarborough, I collect," he said, and could not keep the note of hope entirely from his voice.

"I think not!" came the dashing response. "Since I find you home, it would be everything foolish to push on to Scarborough and the dullest party in the world, don't you agree?"

Whatever else, he was beginning to know that *this*

was not destined to prove a dull gathering: the mere thought of it threw him into a panic. "Oh, but Lady Eleanor will be in expectation of your coming, surely? And, well, I have my sister and her husband staying here, and I must own they are a lamentably dreary pair." In the most craven way he went on: "How would it be if you were to fulfil your engagement at Scarborough and then favour us with a visit on your way home? I could fix for you to meet our acquaintances in the neighbourhood at a series of small gatherings." In fact, aside from these excuses, he was reflecting that it really was time the family entertained again now that the period of mourning for his father was over.

"Nonsense!" said Miss Rishworth with a sparkling smile. "I am persuaded your sister and I will deal excessively well together—I invariably take my own sex in liking." She broke off while he succumbed to a brief fit of coughing. "As to your friends, I am sure I have no wish to put your mother to the trouble of formal entertaining."

"And Lady Eleanor?" he protested feebly; but knowing full well the battle was lost.

"Eleanor must manage without me for once."

Sir Ranulf accepted defeat with dignity and rang for the housekeeper. Mrs Chart, who had just been told by Mr Headcorn of the chilly response the young lady's arrival had occasioned in the master, was astonished to be informed now that a room was to be made ready for her. ". . . And so I will leave you in Mrs Chart's capable hands, Miss Rishworth."

He was conscious of the need to see his mother without delay and inform her of her new guest's presence in the house; and he had hastily rejected the idea of leaving Helen alone in the Little Drawing Room when he bethought him of the treasures it contained that she might casually handle. He turned again to the housekeeper. "Miss Rishworth has had a hot, tiring day on the road and I am sure she will appreciate the chance to rest and refresh herself." Whereupon he moved in haste towards the door, but was not surprised to hear Helen's voice raised in protest behind him: "No, really—I had much rather stay here!" And, for the first time, Miss Rishworth now contrarily sat down.

Mrs Chart fixed her bulging orbs upon the visitor in a look of severe disapprobation at this open flouting of Sir Ranulf's wishes. "This way, miss, *if* you please," she said. Sir Ranulf then held open the door, Mrs Chart sailed out through it, and Miss Rishworth —looking faintly disconcerted—had little choice but to do as she was bid on that occasion.

Lady Thrinby took the news of the arrival of her future daughter-in-law with a calm which astonished her son. As she went to dress for the momentous dinner she told him: "I shall do my best to get that vexatious gal of mine to keep a curb on her tongue for once, depend on it."

But Sir Ranulf was not reassured on that head: no one exercised that degree of control over Letty, not even her mama. He, on the other hand, seemed to have been rendered dumb all of a sudden by the turn of events. Ever since he had crossed the threshold a week ago, hoping for a much-needed rest, he had been forced to grapple with one facer after another; the

Thrinbys' famous decisiveness seemed to have entirely deserted him.

He had to own that the difficulties all stemmed from Gordon's presence (or absence) there. Without him, Letty would not have been quite so viperish, and nor would Miss Rishworth's arrival be such an embarrassment. Gordon was not the kind of boy to be hidden quietly in the house, he knew that well enough now; in fact, in order to extract a promise from him that he would not abscond again, various undertakings had been given with regard to horses and riding. Consequently the lad now spent far more time in the stables than under the eye of the demoralized Miss Hibbert, and he himself gave him a daily riding lesson. It was spoiling him, and no way to rear a youngster in an unindulgent world, but until such time as permanent provision was made for him, he was taking no chances. His unruly ways were only to be expected of a child with no discipline or schooling, and it was not wonderful that he should have hankered for the gypsy life. However, his disappearance had been a near-run thing and it had shaken his protector a good deal.

Had Gordon not been run to earth that day, he might indeed have been compelled to call upon the Priory; but as it was he had not seriously considered carrying out his threat. For one thing he had not told his mother of the de Hyville girls' involvement, and he did not know how she would view any unnecessary association in that quarter after all these years of aloof belligerence. Of course the quarrel had always stemmed primarily from his father and was directed at Sir John Huggins—as he had persisted in calling him: only a dashed loose screw would change a perfectly good English name like that to an outlandish one such as de Hyville, he was used to say. But after all, they *were* neighbours; and Sir Ranulf's conscience smote him a little for not letting the two ladies know that Gordon was safe.

He was still standing lost in thought by the window of his mother's room when Headcorn entered. "A message from the stables, sir—your horse will be saddled in five minutes."

Sir Ranulf stared at him in a bemused fashion. "But I didn't ask—"

"No, sir: but the young gentleman grows impatient, I understand," Headcorn said with one of his rare smiles.

"Ah, Gordon! It slipped my mind—yes, it must be high time for his lesson—very well."

Alone again, it struck him that there was little sense in repining over lack of courtesy to the Miss de Hyvilles when he had Helen Rishworth under his roof; since that lady was plainly going to take most of his attention for the foreseeable future. But now, instead of changing for dinner he went off resignedly to don his riding boots.

By the time he returned to the stables—and because Gordon was an apt pupil time tended to fly during his lessons—Letty's carriage was once again standing in the yard. The sight filled him with foreboding. He had been vaguely half-hoping for Providence to intervene in the form of a broken perch or trace—since a pressing invitation from Lord Ailesbury for the Beckforths to stay overnight at Jervaulx was not an altogether dependable likelihood in his

142

opinion. Feeling convinced that this was to be one of the most harrowing evenings he had ever faced, he walked slowly back to the house.

He no longer employed a valet, having grown tired of endless arguments, with an overbearing coxcomb twice his own age, as to what he should wear. No doubt he had been a trifle unlucky in inheriting one such as Carnes from his father, but the experience had cured him of valets of any kidney for the present at least. The fact that it was taking him an inordinately long time to dress for dinner now had little to do with his lack of a valet, however. He paid Weston of Old Bond Street a great deal of money to make his coats, which meant that he need spend as little time as possible in shrugging into them: for Weston's coats were of an irreproachable standard—bar a crease in the linings sometimes which even Brummel had not regarded—and enabled the wearer to dispense entirely with the services of a valet. (Or so, at any rate, Sir Ranulf chose to believe.) His cravats were all unambitious and a matter for equal celerity—though not this time, he thought crossly, discarding his third attempt. This sudden onset of perfectionism was not, he realized guiltily, because he aimed for an exquisite effect with which to dazzle his lady downstairs, but simply to delay his appearing before her until the last possible moment. Taking up a fourth neckcloth with a sigh, he calculated that Miss Rishworth must have made Letty's acquaintance by now. Still more guilt assailed him as he felt that he should already be at her side, protecting her from the vicious verbal assault that would most certainly be coming her way . . .

That thought made him hurry—and proceed more slowly still. But at last he was ready, sartorially if not mentally, and he made his way with resolute tread to the Great Drawing Room. The footman opened the door before him and he braced himself for raised voices and empurpled faces—or perhaps an icy silence. But instead, the scene which he entered into was all civility and punctilio.

His gaze went to Miss Rishworth first; which was not surprising as she was wearing a sumptuous satin and tulle dress with a scarlet bodice and green skirt. He could not recall seeing it before—or anything as elegant—at any of their Town engagements, and he elevated Scarborough society considerably in his mind: it must be very high ton indeed. Those contrasting colours were fashionable, he knew, and there was no denying the style vastly flattered her blonde looks.

Laetitia, who had not known of Miss Rishworth's presence when she was dressing for dinner, was nonetheless not wholly outshone. Her own taste verged on the gaudy and was well-suited by the current rage for violet and primrose, which she had chosen now. She was standing next to Helen and conversing, as far as he could tell, with perfect amiability! Even brother-in-law Beckforth had set aside his book for the moment, and was evidently making a push to be gallant to Miss Rishworth. His mother, seated in her usual place, threw him a knowing look as he approached the group and murmured his apologies.

His arrival naturally banished the incipient smile from Letty's face, but Miss Rishworth bore down upon him with a cheerful greeting; almost as if she were mistress of Thrinby Hall already.

"Sir Ranulf, there you are! Your sister has been telling me about Jervaulx Abbey—such a quaint place it sounds! If the weather still holds tomorrow we are quite set upon an expedition there."

"But you have this minute returned from Jervaulx, have you not?" he applied to Laetitia in bewilderment. "Ailesbury will think you mean to take up residence!"

Her cheeks fired and she drew breath for one of her most blighting answers, but Miss Rishworth, with a sharp look at them both, continued smoothly: "Papa has known Lord Ailesbury for ever, and I am perfectly sure he will be all smiles when I call there with acquaintances."

Sir Ranulf could not but admire this effortless handling of Laetitia: for her to be silenced and relegated to an acquaintance, in one short languid sentence, was finishing indeed. He said: "Are you party to this new scheme, Beckforth? I inquire only in a spirit of curiosity as to the transport, you understand." His tone was not overtly quizzical and was lost upon everyone except his mother, whose eyes twinkled appreciatively.

Again Helen Rishworth took command. "Your sister and I will use my travelling carriage and Mr Beckforth will ride with you, Sir Ranulf."

"Ah, I am to come too, am I?— how very pleasant," he murmured. "And whose horses?"

"Ours!" cried Laetitia, in the manner of one playing a winning trump at last from a miserable hand.

"Ah," he said once more, and was about to turn the subject when Helen forestalled him.

"I have been *so* admiring the things in this room, and am all impatience to ask you about them."

His heart sank as another Egyptian discourse loomed: while the apartment was by no means as Memphian in style as the Little Drawing Room, quite a few of his father's old mementoes mingled uneasily with the Jacobean furnishings. "Oh, some other time, I think," he demurred.

"Ranulf! So churlish to our guest!" Letty hooted at once; and in no time he found himself staring fixedly at the Egyptian lyre, and listening to a lengthy eulogy upon it.

A gleam of humour entered his bored eyes, and he walked over and took up the instrument, saying: "It is even more fascinating than you suppose, Miss Rishworth—for here we are presented with an almost unique chance to hear the actual sounds familiar to the ears of the Ancients."

"Truly? You mean it still works?" she asked eagerly, missing his irony.

"To be sure it does." He took the lyre across to his mother, holding it out to her and continuing, tongue in cheek: "Alas, this will enforce our silence for a little while, but I'm persuaded you will think it worth it since Mama knows how to touch this with such sweet, infinite pathos as you never heard in all your life . . ."

Knowing full well her son's real opinion of her efforts upon the old lyre, Lady Thrinby here favoured him with a look that spoke volumes. "Ranulf!"

146

Letty's corncrake rang out again. "How thoughtless to ask poor mama to play before dinner!"

But before a brangle could develop between the musician's children, over the abstruse point as to the propriety of playing Egyptian lyres before or after dinner, Headcorn intervened with the announcement of the meal itself. Not even Helen proposed that her ladyship should play to them at the table, although by this time Sir Ranulf would not have been greatly astonished had she insisted on it—and had her way.

To his immense relief there were no further disputations during dinner, although Miss Rishworth continued to dominate the talk. He noticed even Letty was regarding their guest with an odd sort of admiration; and could only wonder at anyone who was able to induce such a response in his virago of a sister. Gradually he began to look on Helen with new eyes—and be filled with admiration himself.

Ten

Sir John de Hyville regarded his heir, who had returned home from Town the day previously, with some exasperation. John, unaware of this scrutiny, continued to gaze dotingly upon his new curricle and waited to hear its praises sung.

"Waste of blunt!" Sir John opined brutally. "What was wrong with the four-wheeled phaeton I let you have, eh?"

Dismayed but undeterred, the young man tried to explain certain elementary facts to his backward-minded parent. ". . . And you see this is much safer than the phaetons, sir, because it is hung *lower* due to these new elliptic springs: and, because of the new suspension, the whole vehicle can be made much lighter—making it easier on the horses," he added, in an attempt to appeal to his father's well-known compassion for animals of all sorts—from quadrupeds down to the smallest of insects.

But Sir John remained unimpressed. "Rattle to bits inside six months, I'd dare swear . . . You'd have done better purchasing a pair of machiners than this fanciful heap of metal: at least they'd give years of faithful service!"

In fact John had bought some horses at the same time as acquiring the carriage, but as he had used them only for the first stage from London they were stabled on the road awaiting his return journey. He deemed it best not to mention them now, and risk further admonishments and advice. "Let me take you for a drive, sir," he said coaxingly; for he was longing for an excuse to demonstrate the gleaming equipage. "We could run out to Ripon, if you like."

"Why the deuce should I like to do that? Besides, I'll go bail that's a deafening brute to ride in, and you know I can't abide noisy carriages, be they never so frippery-smart!"

Unfortunately this latter objection was unanswerable: John had found it to be a bit of a grinder himself, and that was his only disappointment with the curricle. That his father should be shrewd enough to discern that just by looking at it, whereas he had not been, annoyed him. Not but what he knew very well that beneath all the romantical and eccentric notions, his father was a very sharp-witted and astute man: indeed he must have been, to have augmented his inheritance by investing as he had; though people tended to forget that sometimes as, for so long now, he had only been interested in his precious Improvements.

However, since coming down from university only a year ago, John had been reminded of his father's acuteness more than once. Whenever he put forward a splendid scheme to him (especially one involving investment) Sir John would go straight to its weak-

150

nesses and, more often than not, explode the whole notion. This had not always hurt him, but his greatest ambition had been, and still was, to build bridges. His father had poured scorn on that proposal from the outset, maintaining that bridge building was mere artisans' work and that *he* was a gentleman. This last point was quite irrelevant to one such as John; he still wished to design bridges, at the very least. But, because he of course thought in terms of the modern iron bridges, that scheme too was summarily dismissed.

"Well, I can't waste any more time inspecting your extravagances," Sir John said impatiently. "Come, and I'll show you the progress—if you can call it that —at the Grotto."

That invitation dispelled John's buoyant mood in a trice. Giving the curricle a look of lingering regret he followed his father out into the sunlight.

He, conversely, was now much more cheerful. "Since you are here, my boy, I'd be obliged for your advice on underpinning the excavation, so that we may contrive to avoid another disaster like last week's."

John assented, with a polite show of interest, though his thoughts remained elsewhere. As the two strode from the coach-house to the upheaval by the river, he said tentatively: "I collect you have not reconsidered buying into the Strand bridge, sir?"

Sir John grinned, saying: "Hah! You're a sticker, I'll say that for you! How could I change my mind, since the facts remain the same? It's a damned costly bridge, to my way of thinking. I can't see tolls there gleaning a *fraction* of a million pounds, now can you, honestly?"

"Well, I—"

"Good God, boy, it's flanked by Blackfriars and Westminster, free bridges both! Any nodcock in that pot will be burned black . . . I only hope you've not thrown away your own money in spite of my warning you off."

"Oh no, sir," John was able to reply with glum honesty. All his instincts had craved owning a portion of such a fine enterprise, but he had respected his father's judgement on the matter. Changing the subject—at least by his own lights—he said: "But would you not like to see it, father? When I return to Town, what say you to coming up with me?"

This proposal, though neatly arrived at, was not quite spontaneous, in that he had assured his sisters that he would do all he could to remove Sir John from the scene in case their irate neighbour came a 'calling.

"I see your game, sir! You're trying to lure me into that modish waggon of yours by fair means or foul!"

John protested, and urged the visit once more, but soon saw that it stood no chance. He repeated as much to Isabella later in the day.

"It doesn't excite my astonishment in the least," she told him. "Papa needs a much stronger inducement than a bridge to leave home these days, but thank you for trying at least."

For his own part, though, John was not really sorry he had failed in that design. It was not in fact convenient for him to bear off his father to London, just to suit the girls' odd kick-ups. In any case he had hit on a plan of his own for dealing with Sir Ranulf Thrinby; and a rather better one than having to suffer a starched-up call from him, with or without their papa in attendance.

He considered that no one could blame Thrinby for *feeling* starched-up, in the deplorable circumstances that had been made known to him; for it was clearly beyond anything that Bianca should lose this small boy in such hoydenish style, and then do nothing to ascertain the fate of the child or even tender an apology. But seeing that both his sisters were now helpless in the affair, he had resolved to set matters aright by calling squarely upon Sir Ranulf himself. He knew that no sensible purpose would be served by telling that to the girls, for they would then be bound to set up a screech.

Not even to himself did he entirely own that there was another reason why he wished to call on the Thrinby family. He still felt a nagging curiosity as to the identity of the Vision who had asked him the way there: for some reason that his scientific mind could not quite define, she had made a devilish deep impression on him; so much so that he felt he could not rest easy about her until at least he had discovered her name, and whether she was staying at the Hall.

* * *

Sir Ranulf did as he was told and accompanied Helen, Letty and Arthur on their new expedition to Jervaulx Abbey even though this necessitated setting out at a monstrously early hour; or so it seemed to him, as he did not hold to the view that one should work too hard at one's pleasures. However, the organ-

153

ization had been undertaken by Miss Rishworth, with the surprising compliance of his sister. The only factor left unsupervised was his own appearance in the breakfast-parlour betimes, but he was so relieved to see that the pair were dealing well together that he was very ready to play his part within their joint scheme.

At Jervaulx, Helen proved herself as indefatigable a walker as she was a traveller and conversationalist. It appeared that the Earl of Ailesbury was presently engaged in cutting back growth from the extensive abbey ruins, with the final aim of landscaping what had for centuries past been a virtual wilderness. Helen insisted upon pacing out every cloister, every refectory and paving where the monks had trod. Letty and Arthur begged off from accompanying her in this, on the dubious grounds that they had seen every inch of it the day before. Very sensibly, in Sir Ranulf's view, they sat in the ruined Chapter House; Arthur as usual soon deep in a book.

"Living close by such a *fascinating* place you must be familiar with *every aspect* of its history," Helen enthused as they strode around together. "Do tell me —when was the *very* old part built, and by whom?"

He cast her a rather haggard glance. "I fear I must disappoint you—since I am by no means an encyclopaedia of historical facts. I suppose the Earl could oblige you with such details." (But he, wise man, was no doubt still at his breakfast.) "Failing that you could have recourse to my brother-in-law, who is often a mine of, er, absolute gems."

"But I'd hazard they are usually on a topic which captivates his audience not in the slightest!"

154

"You may well be right there," he said, with a faint smile, although he was disconcerted at her ruthlessness in so demolishing poor Arthur: and on such a short acquaintance, too, he reflected.

They tramped past the endless heaps of masonry. With the best will in the world he could not endow them with romance at ten-thirty in the morning, but they seemed to afford his companion endless interest. He began dropping behind her brisk pace, though following on with a certain fatalism: there must come an end, after all, even to the Jervaulx ruins.

"You know, by the greatest good fortune I have my water colours with me," Helen told him presently when he caught her up again. "I shall be able to spend some happy hours here with my brushes."

He wondered uneasily whether she referred to to-day, the immediate future, or such time as when she was in residence as Lady Thrinby. Their ambiguous relationship was beginning to disturb him: the fact that he had not actually proposed to her yet was, he suspected, a detail fast becoming superfluous. He recalled with further unease the several baskets and paraphernalia which had been strapped to her carriage. "Er, you intend to set up your easel without delay, then?"

"No, not now—imagine it on a clear dawn!—*that* is when it should be captured!"

Aghast at the prospect of dawn expeditions, he said: "But Helen, there are castle ruins aplenty nearer my home." And to those words he added a silent prayer that they all might lack the *je ne sais quoi* that would appeal to her in the aurora light.

But her reply was inexorable. "Then you must take me to see them *all*."

"I shall be delighted," he replied, wooden-faced.

This point established, they continued their tour in thoughtful silence for a little while. "Sir Ranulf," Helen said presently, "I am sure I may speak to you in all frankness?"

Wondering what in the world was coming next, he besought her to continue.

"Only I thought it would make matters *so* much more comfortable between us if I told you now that your sister has acquainted me with details regarding the boy."

The devil she has, he thought, momentarily at a loss for an answer. They now walked along a broad grassy path, and hitherto Helen had been the one who stopped periodically to admire a vista and set it mentally in a frame; but this time he checked, saying in a way that was more challenging than he had intended: "The boy?"

Helen here cast a look of deep compassion upon him. "Yes: I apprehend it is a matter of some *délicatesse*, and I daresay you will not wish to discuss at length with me. I merely wanted you to know that I am no green girl—nor am I easily shocked."

And with another grave smile she walked on ahead again. Sir Ranulf hurried after her, exclaiming: "Now look here, I—!"

"One sees now, of course, why you were a trifle flurried by my arrival, but you have no cause, believe me."

"No, indeed I have not!" he declared with vehemence.

"Quite so," she continued in the same tone of cloying sympathy. "By all accounts he is the most delightful child. I divined from your sister's remarks that she may not herself be over-fond of children, but I *adore* them, and perhaps more so if they show a little spirit—which this boy has in plenty if his recent pranks are anything to judge by. Oh yes! Mrs Beckforth told me the whole—I was *aux anges* over it all!"

"I doubt that Laetitia—"

"But it is perfectly plain to me that the child stands in need of a settled home—do say that I may be permitted to meet him at the earliest possible moment," she concluded, administering a light tap on his wrist that seemed to convey still further depths of understanding.

He scarcely knew where to begin in order to disabuse her of her wildly out conclusions: schooling his anger, he told her bleakly: "I fear you are labouring under a complete misapprehension, brought about by my sister's rather unreliable presentation of the circumstances. The boy is in no way related to me, but because of the peculiar nature of the case I am not at liberty to disclose his identity to anyone—certainly not to Letty. His stay was by my invitation and is a limited one. Indeed, I am in daily expectation of instructions as to where I must take him when his future is arranged."

He had sensed Helen's eyes probing him throughout his speech, and he now met them directly. "That is the truth, Helen, and I am deeply sorry that you were misled, and no doubt distressed, by Letty's mischief-making." Although in fact he was aware that Helen had shown no sign whatever of discomfiture over Letty's tattling; he would rather have wished that she had.

She returned his gaze unwaveringly and said: "Pooh, I was not put out of countenance by such disclosures. *That* was what I wished to convey to you. I should still like of all things to meet the child."

This response to his disclaimer was not what he had hoped for. He had a definite feeling that she did not believe him. He said coldly: "I doubt that any useful purpose would be served by such a meeting. It might unsettle him: he is hard to control at the best of times."

Miss Rishworth jutted her chin. "Then you forbid me to speak to him, is that the case?" she said dangerously.

"Good Lord, no—how melodramatic! But if you reckon to discover his antecedents by that means you will be sadly disappointed. Poor Gordon is quite in ignorance of his parentage beyond knowing that his mother has recently died—his father he has never known."

Helen gave him another deep look that he did not care for, but, to his relief, said no more on the subject. Gordon aside, this talk had borne in on him that Helen plainly saw herself as betrothed; although in fact he had done no more than approach her father in the proper preliminary fashion. Whilst not regarding himself as a stickler for the conventions, or, at the other pole, one given to high flights of romance, he did believe that his formal proposal to the lady of his choice should be of some significance to her. Furthermore, he now had to own to a distinct reluctance to declaring himself to Miss Rishworth: but it was very

158

late in the day for him to have come to that piece of knowledge. In the circles of the Upper Ten Thousand in which they both moved, the match was already an accomplished fact. A fine figure he would cut if he cried off now, and the girl could claim a jilting: not without justification, since he had been crass enough to obtain Rishworth's prior consent.

Thinking of Lord Rishworth took him back to the precise words that his lordship had addressed to him when they were closeted together, and the impression he had received that the blessing had not been vouchsafed with total willingness. At the time he had wondered if the Viscount—a widower—was just a little loth to part with a final, useful unwedded daughter; but now a less selfish reason occurred to him. Rishworth must surely know better than anyone of Helen's managing and independent ways; had there not been a real earnestness in his watery gaze when he adjured him to 'be very sure you intend this offer, Sir Ranulf?' He had taken that for mere punctilio—perhaps with a dash of lordly disdain for his suit. But now it seemed increasingly like . . . spontaneous sympathy.

His dejection deepened still further as he rode back alongside his taciturn brother-in-law in the wake of the carriage. Upon arriving home he excused himself from company with the plea that he had to write letters; in fact, to continue wrestling with his sombre thoughts, safe from Helen's presence until dinner.

But he encountered her again before then: when he went to the stables for Gordon's riding lesson he found her there, resplendent in the palest blue military-style riding habit complete with epaulettes, frogging and a plumed Glengarry cap. To his no small exasperation he had to own all over again that she was remarkably attractive and that her attire, which he had seen before when she rode in Hyde Park, suited her to perfection. Vacillating again in his feelings, he thought that perhaps he had been too severe upon her.

"Letty said I might find you here now, and could petition you for the use of a saddle-horse," she called to him gaily as he stepped through the brick archway.

"Of course," he returned, seeing through Letty's game at once; she had sent Helen down to the yard now knowing full well that Gordon would also be there. But was Helen herself aware of that? Her beautiful face gave nothing away.

While the stablelad fetched a suitable mount for her she said: "I see you intend to ride yourself just now—will you accompany me, for I am very sure I shall else get lost!"

"Gammon! I've seen how you handle a bit of blood before now."

"Yes, you have—when the furthest limit was the Stanhope Gate! In the country, I have the most lamentable sense of direction there ever was!"

Before he could rally her again Gordon came round the stone trough in the corner of the yard, his hand held firmly in the grip of Miss Hibbert's. Whereupon his fair companion gave an artless little cry of pleasure and eagerly approached the child, ignoring his own wry expression.

That particular lesson was a total waste of time. His pupil took crafty advantage of the fact that his attention was frequently distracted, showing off shamelessly before the handsome lady, who poured praise upon him at every naughty caprice. In the end, Gordon galloped off towards a far boundary when his back was turned for a second while he was dismounted to shorten Helen's stirrup. He gave belated chase across the width of the park, with the girl's laughter following after them. It would not take long, he thought, before the two were acting in collusion against him, for in some unscrupulous respects they seemed to have much in common . . .

Next morning, when he entered the breakfast-parlour at the respectable country hour of half-past nine, Letty, Arthur and Miss Rishworth were near to leaving the table. Lady Thrinby always had a tray in her room and did not come down until later, so she was not an observer of the new and invigorating start to each day at the Hall since Helen's arrival.

Arthur favoured him with a morose nod; Letty sniffed; and Helen looked up from salting a muffin and cried in her cheerful way: "There you are, Sir Ranulf!"

He was beginning to recognize this as her customary greeting to him at all times. He found he did not greatly care for it, but, having made a firm over-night resolution to pass over such minor annoyances, he smiled and gave a cordial answer.

"We were hoping you would be down not *too* late today," she said sweetly, "for the carriage will be at the door in—didn't you say within the half-hour, Laetitia?"

Sir Ranulf hastily poured himself some coffee unless it might be snatched away from him, and asked a pained-looking Headcorn for fresh toast. Then he re-plied with due caution: "Will it, indeed?"

"Of course—you must remember we go to Foun-tains Abbey this morning?"

"No, I don't remember: which may be because I was not told, you know," he said with another con-scientious smile.

Helen frowned. "Weren't you? It was certainly gone into at length—though wait!—I collect that Letty and I decided for it when you were over the port. Never mind!" she told him buoyantly, "you did say, did you not, that you would be pleased to show me all over the local places of Gothic times?"

He felt temper rising within his breast, quite extin-guishing his good resolution, but said in a controlled tone: "I should be happy to in the ordinary way, but on this occasion I regret I shall not be able to accom-pany you anywhere."

"But you must!" Helen's voice had risen with her colour; she seemed annoyed at this sign of indepen-dence on his own part.

"And I have just told you that I can't. I have some calls that must take precedence. I am sorry, but there it is. If you desire my company another day, it would be wise—and considerate—to ask me before I am put upon a carriage like a human bandbox!"

He was at once taken aback by his own tart words, which were so at variance with what he had intended saying to Helen this morning. He had planned to show her the estate which was to be hers, until she had set him on his high ropes with this absurd command.

"You *do* surprise me, Ranulf," Letty now struck

in. "For I cannot *think* of the last time you troubled youself to pay a call in the neighbourhood."

"No? Well, you are not here quite all the time," he countered wickedly.

He could tell from past experience that an outrageous answer was forming on her compressed lips. But before she could utter it, Helen interposed with an air of offended dignity: "Perhaps those of us who intend seeing the abbey should prepare to leave now."

"You are very right, my dear," Letty agreed; mimicking Helen's well-bred restraint somewhat awkwardly, since it was not in her usual line. "*Arthur!*—come along."

Sir Ranulf, left hunched at the table, was given further food for thought by the exchange. He saw, among other things, that Helen and Laetitia were a redoubtable pair in harness, and made a definite decision that his sister would not cross the threshold after they were married.

When he could no longer hear the carriage wheels he fell to wondering listlessly how to occupy his morning; for of course he had no real calls which were incumbent upon him to pay.

Then he remembered that was not quite the case.

Eleven

Having formed the unprecedented intention—for a de Hyville—to visit Thrinby Hall, John did not allow himself too much time to ponder upon the wisdom of his action. The very next day he set off for the Hall at noon; the earliest conformable hour for a morning visit; although whether any time at all could be apt for this particular visit was something he would doubtless discover in a very short while, he thought apprehensively as he cantered up their own winding tree-hung drive, which was narrowed almost to a tunnel in places during the summer.

About a hundred yards from the gate he rounded a bend so overgrown that it permitted only single file—and came smash up against another gentleman on horseback. He had been too immersed in his own thoughts to have heard his approach. As it was, both reined in and eyed the other in wary silence until Sir Ranulf announced himself.

John was quite confounded. "Oh—ah—yes—John de Hyville."

In manoeuvring close enough to shake hands each

had time to consider his next words, which were delivered simultaneously.

"Extraordinary thing! After all these years I was just—" said John.

"I beg you will forgive this intrusion after—" said Sir Ranulf.

They both laughed with mutual embarrassment, and John felt encouraged by the Baronet's unbogey-like aspect to address him frankly. "I was this minute on my way to the Hall in the hope of seeing you." —And, with any luck, the mysterious Hebe you have there, he added to himself. He determined to do his utmost now to be cordial to Sir Ranulf, so that perhaps a more formal visit could be arranged later. In order to achieve this purpose he was cheerfully ready to sacrifice Bianca's good name. "The fact is, I was dashed anxious to tender you my sincere apologies for the havey-cavey conduct of my young sister towards your, er, ward." He coloured a little and continued hastily: "Is he safe now, by the by?"

"Yes, the young rip! What a dance he has led us all! But never mind that—I fear I have been most remiss in waiting until now to set your sisters' minds at rest about him."

"How so?—it's no more than they deserve," said John with dispassion. "Why, if they'd played a start like that on me I'd have—I'd have—"

Sir Ranulf grinned and said mildly: "No, there was not a great deal one could do in the event, was there? How is the younger one's foot now?"

"Oh, Bianca is in high gig again, but she was in a rare pucker over the lad until it seems they heard his voice again coming from your grounds."

"Ah! the notorious banshee wail: how unneighbourly of us to inflict it upon you! I gather it is his particular pleasure to hide in a tree, pretend he is a monkey or somesuch creature, and emit the curious noise you speak of. Sometimes it is worse than others —on the occasions he falls from the branches! Still, I am glad of it for the first time if it served to inform your family of his return." Sir Ranulf's expression grew more serious. "I don't excuse myself from all blame in the matter. Would it be possible for me to see your sisters and try to explain? But if you, or they, would rather I desisted you have only to say so. Tell you the truth, de Hyville, I find myself in a deucedly odd position coming here at all, after a lifetime of ignoring your very existence through parental decree!" His mount shifted restlessly beneath him, as if sensing the unease he spoke of.

"God, I know exactly how you feel!" replied John with quick sympathy. "I was in the liveliest dread of calling on you for the self-same reason. Why *is* there this sad Montague and Capulet affair between us, sir? My father has never properly explained and it was all long before my day."

"The *tracasserie* is none of my doing," disclaimed Sir Ranulf with an eloquent shrug. "These old men . . ." Whatever he thought of the actions of the old men he let hang in the air.

"A dev'lish rum start," said John more bluntly. "But I don't see why we should let it stand in *our* path, do you, sir?"

"No indeed—well spoken! But I daresay Sir John won't be brought round to see it in the same light."

Recalling some of the harsh words that his father

had uttered over the years, John had to agree that a full reconciliation was unlikely. "But I'm dashed if you shan't see the girls now that you're here—look, I'll take you to the old dairy, and then I'll send 'em to see you there."

Although it did sound improbable that Sir John, with his consequential airs, would condescend to frequent an old dairy, nevertheless Sir Ranulf could not quite like this furtive arrangement. "But is that not a grave risk for me to run?" he said lightly, smiling. "I mean to say—if I, of all people, were found at a clandestine rendezvous with a Miss de Hyville!"

"Oh, I shall be there too," John assured him with a certain bravado; although in truth he did not care to dwell himself upon such a scene if his father should intrude on it. But he knew he spent pretty well all his time now near that stupid grotto, and that there was scant danger of his straying from there. "Besides, this is a famous place for playing least in sight—we could lose the Tenth Hussars in here to a man, as you'll see." He turned his horse off the drive and led the way down a side path.

Sir Ranulf took his point as he gazed in wonder at the rocky promontories, the excavated hollows which had formed them, and the artfully planted groves of trees. He caught glimpses of the occasional Gothic turret and tower sprouting from minor edifices here and there, but the Priory itself remained hidden from sight for the moment.

He was led to one of these buildings in the grounds, and gazed at it in surprise as he halted his animal by John's. The mortar between the stones appeared fairly new, despite the contrary evidence of quaint arched windows and a cloak of encroaching ivy which straggled up to its romantically toppling pinnacles. "A cottage *orné*?" he ventured.

"No, this is the old dairy," said John matter-of-factly. "You'd best tie your gelding inside here." He left his own horse to graze and walked through a gaping and ragged hole in the end of the building.

"My God!" ejaculated Sir Ranulf when he had followed him. "I beg your pardon—but I have never seen a dairy like this one before!"

"No: and it has never seen a milk churn, I promise you that!—or at least, not one containing milk! As you see, it is 'old' in name alone. Father has littered the whole park with these monstrosities in the mode of the Druids! Then there is the house itself, which makes Fonthill seem like a neat villa, I dare swear! There was a perfectly good new house on this site in the first place, as I expect you know: foursquare, roomy, and with a fine plain front, judging from prints I've seen of it. But there—" He broke off and shrugged. "You'll be telling yourself m'father really is out in his cock-loft just as yours doubtless said he was—but he ain't, Sir Ranulf, mark my words. When his mind's off the past, he's as shrewd as can hold together, as downy a one as you're ever likely to meet."

Hardly reassured by these further disclosures, the visitor inquired tentatively: "And does he know of his daughter's escapade with the boy?"

"No, that all fell out in the most fortunate fashion." John went on to explain that his parent believed merely that their neighbour had come to the girls' aid when Bianca took a tumble out riding.

Sir Ranulf chuckled. "Your sisters are downy ones too, it seems."

"When it suits 'em," said John with brotherly candour. "Well, I'd better be off and tell 'em you're here —I'll be back in a crack!" He strode outside and swung up to his saddle.

Sir Ranulf tied his mount conveniently to what he supposed was a false cow-ring set in one of the walls. Then he skulked about in the make-believe dairy, feeling ridiculously like a fugitive from justice.

A smile touched his lips at the thought that he had declined in such positive terms to see Fountains Abbey today, but had still found himself amongst ruins of a sort, even though these were sham. He peered out through the (presumably genuine) cobwebs across the solitary small window. The scene outside looked quite eerie, apart from de Hyville's fantasies, for clouds were gathering in the midday sky and there was the oppressive silence which heralded a summer storm.

He wondered what he would do if *Père* de Hyville did by chance come to inspect this particular folly, and found a mortal foe crouching inside. But there seemed to be no real reason why he should, since the little place was apparently not even used for storage purposes. He began to feel very foolish to be waiting there.

But it was not long before he heard voices and then caught sight of the sisters' white dresses and colourful shawls as they approached. John was with them and all three were on foot. A few seconds later Isabella was saying to him: "Sir Ranulf, what *must* you think of us, receiving you in this shabby style!—and

170

this is quite an historic occasion, after all!" For John had explained that the Baronet was not here seeking retribution for past—or even present—offences against him.

"Yes, and as I have no desire for it to prove too memorable, I am quite content to hide in the dairy, I assure you! Do come in, I believe it may rain." He stepped aside so they could enter. " 'Servant, Miss Bianca—and how is your ankle now?"

That young lady had not felt any keen desire to encounter Sir Ranulf once more, even after John's assurances that his manner was *très benin*. "Better, I thank you," she murmured, avoiding his amused eye. "I—I want you to know how *tremendously* sorry I am for what I did. I know it was wrong—Gordon is safe and well now, I collect?" She forced herself to regard him.

"There is not the slightest call for apology on that head. After only a brief association with Gordon I find I can feel for your predicament that day very well. Yes, he is his old self again," he assured her, smiling over her shoulder at Isabella. "Mind you, he was a shade downcast when I caught up with him— the only time I have seen him so."

"Did you have great difficulty?" Isabella asked.

"No, I ran him to ground that same night, with no chase whatever: you might say the scent was breast-high! For you see I went straightway to the parish constable at Ashbeck"—(Bianca here paled at the very mention of that personage)—"and found that the worthy fellow had the rascal under lock and key! In a cell that would have kept in a dancing bear—would that I had just such a cage at the Hall!" he interpolated feelingly. "Well, as you may imagine, the constable was vastly pleased to see me, as he was *getting to know* Master Gordon by then, and could make no sense of his story whatever.

"But what had happened was this—as far as I've been able to piece it together. After he slipped from the chaise at your friend's house at Ashbeck he ran for some distance along the road—away from the route taken by the carriage, of course. Then he had what appeared the good fortune to meet with a farmer driving home from market, with a cartful of mouth-watering fruit. This presented the runaway with his two most pressing needs at that time—food and transport."

Bianca nodded with fervent sympathy; despite everything that had happened her eyes moistened at her recollection of the boy's hunger.

"Now this is where the tale becomes garbled: and the constable didn't credit a word of it, though for my part I'm not so sure." Sir Ranulf paused to give Bianca a speaking look. "Gordon told him that he tendered a guinea to the fruit fellow in exchange for food, a lift to Ripon, and a large sum in change—well, in boyish eyes at least!"

"Why to Ripon?" asked Isabella in a failing voice.

"I think that was where he fancied he would join his intended bosom-bows—the wretched gypsies. But it was not to be. Instead, he learned a useful lesson about human nature. For the good farmer, no doubt unable to believe either his eyes or his luck, pocketed the coin, thrust the boy into the ditch and drove away."

That last intelligence drew a cry of anguish from

172

Bianca; but not for the reason her sister supposed. She wailed: "But that was *my guinea*!"

Her brother, who for some reason had not been apprised of that detail of the story, here interjected with severity: "You nodcock! To put that much blunt into a lad's hands!"

"I *didn't*! He . . . stole it." She glanced under her lashes at Sir Ranulf, wretched to have to lay this accusation against her fallen angel. "Well, that is to say, he took it from me in a game we played, and it was not until much later I apprehended—"

"Oh, not to put too fine a glaze on it I think we can say he stole your money. But when someone else took it from *him*, then his righteous anger knew no bounds! So much so that he knocked up the next cottage he came to and demanded to be told the whereabouts of the nearest constable, who incarcerated him as I said: not solely because of the preposterous tale which the worthy youthful complainant set before him, but also as he declined in the most violent way to give his name and direction." Sir Ranulf's tone here lost its note of irony and became sombre. "And so he was detained—for which we all have reason to be glad."

John, who was realizing that he had not been told the half of this fustian before now, gave a grunt of fraternal disgust. His sisters began murmuring their regrets once more but Sir Ranulf brushed them aside. "In the event it was a fidge over nothing at all. Had I been less tired from travelling at the time I wouldn't have browbeaten the pair of you as I did. I came here now to *give* an apology, not to receive one."

When that topic was done with at last, an awk-

173

ward silence lay between the quartet standing in the odd little building. Even John, who bore the least burden of conscience, and who had a sly reason of his own for wishing to foster civility between the two families, was at a loss as to how to go about it in such circumstances; for how could one butter up a guest whom one had to keep confined in a folly to protect him from one's feuding parent?

Sir Ranulf, too, was at a stand to know how to prolong this unusual meeting, which he was finding rather pleasurable in spite—or perhaps because—of its singular nature.

A distant roll of thunder then filled this hiatus, and Bianca exclaimed at once: "I must go to Mama— you know she cannot abide a storm." This was true: though it was also an admirable excuse for her quitting the Baronet's presence, in which she could still not be quite easy.

"Yes, you go back to the house, love," Isabella said, understanding her feelings. "Draw your shawl over your head in case it suddenly pours."

The coming storm was a clear signal for the other three to part company, but it seemed they shared a mutual reluctance to do so. Sir Ranulf did speak of leaving but John answered: "I should out-wait the rain, sir. I know this place looks as if it would leak like a sieve, but father made it weather-tight as well as quaint." He was looking up at the sky out of the grimy window.

Sir Ranulf turned to Isabella. "Do thunderstorms throw you into a quake, ma'am?"

"No, not at all—I've inherited Papa's tendency

174

rather than my mother's although I lack his positive relish for them!"

"A relish for tempests . . . That is uncommon, certainly, but then, if I may say so, he seems to be a most uncommon man," he said seriously and without his usual rather sardonic inflexion.

"Oh, he is! He is driven by this—well, I was about to say *hobby horse*, but it is really more than that: he has an obsession for everything Gothic and, as he sees it, sublime. Storms he regards as highly sublime!"

"Yes, I see—I think! But does it not become somewhat trying, all this constant Sublimity in your everyday life?"

Isabella considered for a moment. "I am so used to it, I suppose, and he is such a dear—not in the least enveloped in mediaeval gloom as one might think."

This polite evasion did not accord with John's more forthright nature. "Yes, it does try me, I can tell you," he grunted from his stance by the window; then, in a changed voice: "Talk of the Devil! There he is now!"

"Where?" cried his sister, rushing over to him.

"No, Bella—keep away, he might see your white dress even through this filthy glass . . . It's the damnable storm that's brought him out of his grotto, confound it!" He spoke rather as if his father were a perverse troglodyte, thought Sir Ranulf who was experiencing a mixture of entertainment and alarm at this latest development. "But if we lay low," John was now saying, "it's still long odds against his coming in here."

As if in mocking heavenly answer to this prediction, there then came a much closer peal of thunder.

The sound frightened Sir Ranulf's horse, which neighed in a manner that seemed deafening to the three of them. Until then they had forgotten the animal's presence.

John groaned. "It's all up, he's heard it . . ." He turned abruptly from the window. "Look, Sir Ranulf, I regret exceedingly that I've placed you in this fix—but leave the talk to me and I daresay we may all brush through it well enough."

The son of the house offered this reassurance in a manner that distinctly lacked conviction. Sir Ranulf nodded with due solemnity, but he had a lively sense of the ridiculous and was hard pressed not to laugh out loud as they all stared mutely at the doorway where the dreaded Sir John was about to make his dramatic entrance. He hoped devoutly a flash of lightning did not accompany this manifestation, as the proceedings would then smack altogether too much of Hamlet's Ghost, and would unquestionably prove his undoing and throw him into helpless fits.

"What in God's name—?" Sir John was now heard to exclaim upon first sighting the horse through the doorway. "*Who goes there*?" he then bellowed ferociously into the depths of the dairy.

John hastened forward, perhaps hoping even now to fend off his approach. "Er, is that you, father?"

There was no portentous lightning, but another clap of thunder, directly overhead, opened the heavens and removed all chance of Sir John remaining outside.

"Of course it's me! But whose is that strange prad?" he demanded looking impatiently over his son's blocking shoulder. He stiffened. "Bella, you

176

here as well?—and good gracious, *who is this*? John—introduce us!"

But it seemed quite beyond the powers of John to pronounce the fateful name of their visitor. Instead, as the rain set up a tattoo on the leaves outside, Isabella said: "Papa, this is Sir Ranulf Thrinby, who has so kindly rid over to see how Bianca goes on after her accident."

Perhaps a full half-minute then passed while Sir Ranulf's pulse beat absurdly in his chest, and while the Eccentric stared at him through the dimness. Then, in something of an anti-climax, the Eccentric merely spluttered out the words: "Has he now!"

However, that brief speech was given in such a way that Sir Ranulf reckoned it would be wise for him to speak out promptly himself. "Yes, I should have called upon you sooner, sir, but to be candid I was not sure that after all this—Believe me, I have not the least desire to embarrass you in any way."

"Eh, embarrass me? How's this?" He rounded upon his son. "John, whatever were you thinking of to bring *one such as Sir Ranulf* in here! I don't wonder at it that he should talk to us of embarrassment!"

The hapless John had become quite bewildered by this further turn of events. His father's demeanour was all at once more toadying than enraged. He did not know what to say, any more than did Isabella.

Sir Ranulf coughed into the prickling silence. "That singularity can be laid at my door: your son and daughter observed me coming down your drive, and immediately made me so welcome that I was encouraged to pursue a wish I have held since boyhood —to see something of your unique achievements with

177

landscaping. And so, when we passed this enchanting building, why, nothing would do for me but to look it over at once!"

He wondered if he had overplayed his hand by such blatant sycophancy; his own father had been obsessed in some degree with his Egyptian interests, and suceptible to boundless praise upon that one subject. But he remembered now that Sir John was said to be shrewd. He felt a sharp renewal of his earlier apprehension.

But Sir John was now beaming all over his still handsome face. "Let me shake your hand, sir! I can see you are a true gentleman—no mushroom like me, eh?—and, even rarer, you possess true *discernment*! I am delighted at last to make your acquaintance!"

Isabella, who had been suffering agonies as she willed him to accept Sir Ranulf, smiled her enormous relief at this verdict. Sir Ranulf himself still did not judge it entirely safe to remove his close attention from the Eccentric, but he caught the warmth of her smile and acknowledged it gratefully with his eyes. Fleeting though it was, to Isabella the look which passed between them signified much more than just his astonishing success with her father. It had also confirmed, with a painful certainty and clarity, that her feelings for this man were stronger than any she had experienced before in her life. Until that moment she had been able to tell herself that she was refining too much upon a natural fascination with their enigmatic neighbour. Now she knew better: and the knowledge gave her pain because, as her father had just reminded her, the de Hyvilles were only mushrooms; in a different world from the Thrinby family.

"This dratted rain!" Sir John was saying, glowering impatiently outside. "You must see the entire scheme of my Improvements—and the house too, of course, Sir Ranulf."

"I can think of nothing that would delight me more, and I don't regard a spot of rain if you do not." That last piece of blandiloquence was rewarded by the rain's sudden abatement. "The storm will add vastly to the sublimity of the surroundings." Now that *must* have gone a step too far with the old boy, he thought with alarm; and another glance at Isabella told him that she feared likewise. But no . . .

"Capital? By God, I take to you more and more! John—do you lead Sir Ranulf's horse to the stables where it ought to be. And Bella—acquaint your mama that she shall receive Sir Ranulf within the hour." He turned back to the visitor. "That is, sir, if I may presume to impose so long upon your time?" And that final complaisance made the brother and sister roll their eyes at each other in amazement at what they were witnessing.

"I count it a great privilege," Sir Ranulf replied humbly. He was now taking a wicked glee in this whole affair, and felt that he hadn't enjoyed himself so much for an age.

Both John and Isabella, for their separate reasons, were just as well pleased; and all the more when their neighbour's triumphant visit culminated in an invitation from Lady Malvina for him to attend her forthcoming moonlight picnic—which had been only a half-hearted scheme until that moment.

Twelve

Sir Ranulf had accepted the invitation with alacrity: what better entertainment for Helen than a moonlight picnic?—and in grounds which were replete with ruins and Gothic fantasies of every description. He was sure that even Helen and Letty would not have arranged any previous engagement for that hour of the night.

When he returned home he found to his relief that the Fountains Abbey expedition was still in progress. He at once sought out his mother to report to her the momentous news of the formal end of hostilities between the Hall and the Priory.

Lady Thrinby had been dozing in her chair when he knocked, and, sensing that her cap was awry, she walked over to the looking-glass to set it to rights. "Where have you been, Ranulf?" she asked him languidly.

A few seconds later her fingers scrabbled convulsively at the cap's quilled lace edging, and she turned her head round to him looking a little wild-eyed. She gave a nervous laugh, saying: "In truth I do believe I'm become a shade hard of hearing lately, just as

Letty keeps saying—I thought *you* just said you have been calling on the de Hyvilles!"

Sir Ranulf smiled as impishly as his thirty summers would allow. "And so I have, Mama! And, you know, it was everything extraordinary and delightful!"

Lady Thrinby forgot about her cap's symmetry and sat down again rather hard. "Tell me about it!" she asked with girlish eagerness; then, in a quite different tone: "What a blessing that your father did not live to see this day, for I'm persuaded it would have killed him . . ."

"Mama, *please*! I have had my fill of maggoty notions today!"

"I am very sure you have—but it would have done, as you must know."

"After the events of this morning I doubt I know anything for certain any longer." And he proceeded to give her an account of them, which included an expurgated version of his first meeting with the de Hyville sisters that made no mention of Gordon's part in it.

She listened in awed silence, finally remarking: " 'Pon my soul! I thought I was past the age of *emotional shocks*, but you have given me what you might term a 'leveller'." A far-off look entered her eyes. "Why, it must be more than a quarter-century since I last saw the Priory. You were still in short coats. It was old Sam Huggins who lived there then, in fact he had built it not long before. Such a cosy, modern place it seemed to me, as a young wife coming from this venerable pile: and such a sensible size," she added wistfully.

182

Her son laughed. "Well, this is by far the cosier of the two now, I think! While as for size, their entrance hall put me much in mind of the north transept of York Minster—though a touch longer and taller and not so snug! Old Sir Samuel's original house may still be there somewhere under the massy masonry, but I didn't see as much as a single honest brick left in sight."

"And you are engaged to go *again*, you say?" She shook her head in stupefaction. "No, I just cannot credit it . . ."

He gave her a gentle smile, comprehending the power of the feud over her mind that she could not believe it was ended. "But I am, for their moonlight picnic: to which you, of course, are most cordially invited if you wish to make up our party. Helen and the Beckworths are asked also, but I did not accept for you in view of—everything."

" '*Of course*', the boy says, as if it were the regular thing for me to be stepping up to the Priory! No, you were right, I shall not go there now. But Helen will doubtless wallow in every last corbel and bastion of it, and cause Sir Johnny Huggins to lose his gentlemanly accents answering all her questions! Ah, poor Sir Johnny Huggins!—your father was always used to call him that—*so* unkind! But what is this you say of taking Letty and Arthur there? Ranulf, if you wish to stay arm-in-armly with the Priory people I would recommend you leave that choice pair behind, *coûte que coûte*."

"But how can I, Mama? They are bound to hear of the invitation through Helen. But of course you are reading my own mind: Letty has always been the strongest of us for the feud now that father is gone. Naturally she'll seize on this chance to go there and be—odious to everyone," he finished quietly.

Here she cast him a deep look. "I am so sorry it has transpired that you've had her burdensome presence to plague you ever since you left Town—and especially once Helen came."

He paused in his answer, through detaching (or trying to detach) a tenacious Priory cobweb from the sleeve of his riding dress. "Yes, I confess it has irked me. But you must have noticed how they seem to live in each other's pockets. Why, I never thought to see Letty deal half so well with anyone—off a broomstick." He gave the cobweb another moody flick.

"Pray cease fiddling with your sleeve!" his mother said peevishly. "Have you asked the Rishworth gal to marry you yet?"

He stared for some seconds at his top-boots. "No . . ."

"Well, I think it high time you did! I do not feel it is on your mind with *sufficient urgency*, Ranulf."

He had to grin at her scolding tone. "Oh, but it is, Mama, you do me an injustice! Look, I give my word that I will request Helen's hand before she returns to Hertfordshire. Now, I cannot say more than that, can I?"

In fact he agreed with her sense of propriety in the matter; it was indeed time for him to cease prevaricating. He would wait his moment only until the picnic, since, whatever might be the sublimity of Sir John's entertainment, the Priory and its surroundings were the very essence of romance, and thus an apt setting for his proposal.

* * *

Had either John or Isabella been privy to this resolve it would have spared them a good deal of ardent speculation during the interval before the picnic; but it would also have deprived them of many pleasurable hopes and dreams. The picnic itself was the subject of endless discourse between them, but neither cared to raise with the other the spectre of Miss Rishworth. Each arrived independently at the cheerful conclusion that that lady was merely a friend of Sir Ranulf's sister.

Bianca's joyful looking-forward to the gathering was unalloyed by any such doubts: Julia and Carleton Amersham had been invited and both had accepted, and it was fixed that they would probably stay at the Priory for a few days afterwards. It seemed that the measles had finally subsided at Ashbeck House. They arrived in the afternoon of the day of the picnic, and when Isabella joined them and Bianca in the drawing-room the talk was mostly concerning matters of raiment: full evening dress was being worn but no jewellery; on the particular advice of Lady Malvina, who, upon the last rustic occasion of this kind had lost a cherished amber brooch somewhere in the gardens, which no amount of searching had ever found.

Isabella thought this restriction was a pity as she greeted the Amershams: Julia's homely looks and sandy colouring needed the glitter of stones to set off her appearance to its best advantage. Her dress of Pomona green crape, in itself very pretty and an admirable choice, revealed an expanse of bare-looking neck and shoulder which fairly cried out for a necklace.

Bianca, on the other hand, with her dark colouring and bright eyes, seemed to lack nothing in her befrilled pink-and-white striped gauze dress. As Isabella well knew, the radiant effect of the whole had its source in the smiling Adonis by her side. What she was not aware of at the time was that Carleton, by a casual reference to the betrothal of a certain golden-haired beauty named Corinna Selsby, had just relieved Bianca's mind of its greatest concern.

"I have been telling Julia and Carleton the sequel to the story of that stupid boy," Bianca said to her with an air of lofty detachment. "Though I've warned them not to breathe a *word* of it to Mama and Papa."

"And what a plucky young lady she is, eh?" observed the handsome Mr Amersham in rallying tones. He had been blessed with wavy auburn hair, beautifully defined eyebrows, and fine-modelled features which were a constant cause of chagrin to his sister. "Imagine carrying off the lad like that from under the Thrinbys' noses, and risking calling down their awful wrath on her pretty head! You know, I ain't so sure I'd be up to snuff for doing that m'self!"

Julia favoured him with a smile which suggested she felt he might well have been so foolish, but Bianca gazed upon her hero with mute gratitude and joy. Her cup was full, and the distress of her adventure at last put behind her.

"We have hired a house in Scarborough so that

mother and the children may recruit after the measles," Julia announced a little coldly; she had not altogether forgotten the nuisance that Bianca's visit had caused her, and wished to speak of something else.

Isabella too was happy to turn to this subject. "Oh yes, that is a splendid notion. Scarborough has been our family's recourse over the years for all manner of disorders—the sea air seems so invigorating. When do you go?"

"The beginning of next month," Julia told her, then laughed ruefully. "I fancy we shall find the conveyance of five young ones and all their goods and chattels to be a debilitating exercise in itself! Poor mother has been thrown into a bustle about the arrangements already, since we no longer keep our nurse-maid, you know: not but what we shall come about in the end, I daresay."

Struck by her friend's tired looks, Isabella said suddenly: "I wonder if Mama would countenance us coming with you—that is, if lodgings could be found in time."

"But of course she would!" cried Bianca in delight, her mind already leaping ahead to a blissful time by the sea when Mr Amersham would be forever at her side.

Julia's eyes had brightened likewise. "Oh *Bella*, do you really suppose it might be contrived? I should like it above all things." Her gaze moved thoughtfully from one sister to the other. "Of course, my dear brother will not be accompanying us, since he is *always* at pains to remove himself from the nursery children whenever he may."

For a second or two it seemed that this acid remark

might capsize the scheme at the outset, but Carleton was quick to refute the suggestion. "Pay no heed to her! Sometimes I think she forgets I am the most devoted brother conceivable! Of course I shall make one of us at Scarborough." Whereupon Julia's expression spoke volumes, but she wisely forebore to comment. It was left that Isabella should approach her mother as soon as an opportunity presented itself.

Before long a great many people were assembled in the Priory drawing-room. The arrangement was for them to foregather in the house before making their way to the al fresco setting of the picnic; in order, as one young wag declared loudly: "To provide one and all with a posset, a hot brick, and a pair of compasses!"

"You'll get no compasses here, Humphrey!" retorted Sir John, who had at that moment joined his guests. "You must travel by the stars tonight, as the Almighty intended, or not at all!"

Half an hour later there was still no sign of the Thrinby party, but at last the buzz of conversation faltered nearer the doors as the butler came in to announce the latecomers. Isabella's heart lightened absurdly as he did so. She was standing close enough to eavesdrop on her parents' greetings, and her rise of spirits suffered a check as she realized that "The Honourable Helen Rishworth" was this very striking fair girl in scarlet and green, possessed of a pair of vivid blue eyes and also a most determined mouth and chin. All her previous doubts and fears rushed back upon her: for if by some evil chance Sir Ranulf's guest was set upon marriage to him, there was not the smallest sign in those fine features that their owner was in the habit of being denied whatever she

188

might desire. She noticed despondingly, as Sir Ranulf led her forward into the body of the room, that those glorious blue eyes swept over him in a way that was distinctly proprietorial. He would need to have windmills in his head to prefer a plain-looking member of a despised and insignificant family to the gorgeous creature at his side.

John, however, eyes alight with recognition of his Fair One, wasted none of his time in similar arid speculation, but assisted his parents in putting the tardy guests at their ease. Not that Miss Rishworth stood in any such need: she was already launched upon a eulogy of the Priory to her astonished and gratified host, who finally murmured: "If you think it well enough now, ma'am—wait until you see it bathed in moonlight!"

Sir Ranulf considered he had been as sycophantic as anyone could be with the Priory's creator when he first met him, and not without good reason; but it seemed that Helen was outstripping him. And yet, he thought fairly, it was not quite sycophancy in her case, but a genuine voracious interest in every subject under the sun—or moon in this instance.

Letty and Arthur were talking apart with Lady Malvina, and Helen seized the opportunity to bombard her host with further questions. He answered these at enthusiastic length, leaving her side with real reluctance when the time came for him to be in readiness at the Greek folly to receive them all there later. "I must be off, ma'am—but my son here knows a good deal about my endeavours to restore the great days of our building heritage—John! I appoint you this lady's guide!" And that willing young gentleman was so pleased by the way things were now falling out that he was even ready—for a time—to sing the praises of his parent's Gothic Mockeries, since Miss Rishworth unaccountably seemed to admire them.

Lady Malvina then drew Isabella into the group, feeling that she herself should be with the other guests. During the following introductions Helen Rishworth merely vouch-safed her a bored nod, being then quite taken up with John's account of some fulsome tracery on a window; Arthur Beckforth bowed without looking at her at all; and Laetitia gave her a demolishing stare and then, like her friend, became interested in the windows, though from a more mundane viewpoint. "How you must regret that those pointed arches do not allow of curtaining," she observed loudly.

Since this subject was not picked up by anybody, she carried it on herself. "Though now I think of it . . . *Come here*, Arthur, and look at these ugly, awkward windows! Tell me if they are not the same sad style of those of your Somersetshire cousins, and would take similar divers draperies? Ah! I thought so! Then I must make known to Lady Huggins what she must do! Pray excuse us . . ."

Isabella nodded blankly, following the pair with her eyes.

"Pay no regard to Laetitia," Sir Ranulf said softly in her ear. "It is just her way. You see, she is forever giving guidance to her hostesses on the ordering of their establishments—whilst abandoning her own snug abode for most of the year."

She gurgled with laughter at this sarcasm, then repressed it. "Well, Mama would be eternally grateful for any advice in rendering *this* house sung, I know! We scarcely ever enter this wing of it in the winter: but perhaps we would, if we could but be directed to the correct Somersetshire curtains?" she added, seeing that his eye was still mischievous.

He chuckled appreciatively. "Oh, undoubtedly you would—but don't imagine her helpfulness would stop there!"

She noticed that John and Miss Rishworth had also now drifted away together, and she was left with Sir Ranulf a little removed from the other guests. She had not seen Bianca for some while, but felt sure that that damsel was still in most dutiful attendance upon the Amersham party.

She knew it was high time for her to make Sir Ranulf known to the other guests, and was about to suggest that to him when, to her great satisfaction, there was a general move out to the gardens. Was she to have the unlooked-for good fortune of his escorting her to the temple? She was very tempted to let it happen as it now so naturally could, but made herself say: "My brother will see that Miss Rishworth is accompanied to the picnic, of course, Sir Ranulf, but if you prefer I will seek them out and we can make our way there together."

But Sir Ranulf saw no need to seek out Helen's company at that moment. He told himself it would be a pity to spoil her evident enjoyment in plying the good-natured Mr de Hyville with her endless questions. Perhaps, with such 'fascinating' concerns talked out of her system, she might be rendered more tranquil by the time he proposed to her later in the evening. To his present restful companion he replied

191

idly: "No, no, they may be halfway to this folly of yours by now." He stared vaguely about him at the small knots of people still left in the room, none of whom he knew by sight.

"Yes, but then there is your sister and her husband," she still felt constrained to remind him. "They will not know the way over the grass."

"Letty and Arthur never go an inch, anywhere, except by carriage, Miss Isabella. And they are not the kind of people who ever get lost." That last remark, and the eloquent sigh that accompanied it, made her giggle again; and caused Sir Ranulf to raise one of his dark eyebrows at her in mock reproof as they passed outside together.

Thirteen

Sir Ranulf had assisted to drape the flower silk Lyons shawl about Isabella's shoulders before they ventured into the dusky Priory gardens.

"You are a seasoned campaigner, I collect, where moonlight pastorals are concerned," he said, indicating her long-sleeved velvet dress, which was indeed rather more substantial than some of the revealing and flimsy creations seen in ghostly form ahead of them as they followed the straggling procession toward the temple.

"Oh no, this will be only my second supper eaten under the stars, as Papa would say, but I do know that July nights in the Dales can be extremely chilly."

He laughed. "And I do *not* know what your papa would say if he heard such sad prosaic stuff—shame on you!"

She led the way through the maze of overhung paths which criss-crossed the park. The sky was still pale with lingering daylight but the moon and an occasional star were already visible. A breeze sounded in the trees and moved the nearby flowers, whose bright colours remained weirdly discernible.

"You know I cannot but marvel at Sir John's achievement in establishing such a variety of plants in this far from congenial climate," he remarked as they strolled between some high banks of heavily scented shrubs.

"Yes, I think it must be the result of the sheer devotion he bestows upon everything here, you know. No power on earth will drag him away from the place as he grows older—but I am wrong to say that! I've just remembered he did express an intention of coming with us in a few days' time to see his first grandchild—though I would still not count on his doing so."

"Could this visit be to the Harrogate sister by any chance?" he asked with a quizzical look, recalling to them both their first encounter over the runaway boy.

"Yes, Hippolita, my elder sister."

"Hippolita?—Bianca?—Isabella?—" he recited slowly. "I have it! Are they not all characters in Mr Walpole's *Castle of Otranto*? But in that case—why no Manfred?"

"Oh, there is!" He could not see her smile but heard it in her voice. "My brother is John Manfred: there, perhaps fortunately, Papa's dynastic sense overbore even his Gothic fervour, and so the John was placed first!"

He was highly amused, declaring: "Then by rights this ought to *be* the Castle of Otranto, for a humdrum word like Priory scarcely does it justice." He had turned round to inspect the facade for a moment. The lofty ramparts and soaring towers were more outrageously romantic than ever against the dark skyline. "Yes, at night-time it is veritably the fiction come alive!"

194

"Oh, Papa would not have hesitated to call it that, I fancy, had not the original name been well established: or perhaps even he felt that might tend to be over-doing matters a trifle."

Sir Ranulf marked the indulgent affection in her tone, and liked her for it. They walked on again as she continued: "Speaking of unusual names, Gordon is one that I have never heard before—that is to say, used as a first name. I must own I rather like it—it has a Scottish ring."

At once she felt the new warmth between them begin to fade. He said: "Yes, I daresay it is a little out of the common run. I cannot comment as to its Scotch derivation."

The words sounded stilted and his tone distant; she felt puzzled, for she had had not the smallest intention of prying, but was not surprised that he now turned the subject. "By the by, after John asked me about our famous feud the other day, I taxed my mother with it. I do not believe there was any great original cause of our parents' antipathy, though one can see a glimmer as to how it began. The two men shared some traits of character—both inherited a secure independence and both tended to be immersed in one subject all their lives. But they were obviously very different in most ways: for example, my father was forever travelling abroad."

"And perhaps he did not appreciate his *genuine* ancestral home as Papa felt he ought?" Isabella interpolated.

"Very likely! Furthermore, when he *was* at home, he was zealous to follow the ordinary pursuits of a country gentleman—whereas Sir John does not, and never has, to my knowledge."

"No, he doesn't. He remains oddly townish in some ways. Why, even now he would not touch a fishing rod, let alone chase the fox."

She had quite shamelessly chosen the longest route to the folly, and there were not many other guests following the same path; but a group of dawdlers now appeared in front of them. Catching sight of them, they both tacitly slowed their own pace.

"Unhappily," he continued, "these differences ensured that the two failed to meet in the usual way, and so when the momentous question of the 'spy tower' arose, quite literally, between them, they were almost complete strangers to each other while being near neighbours."

"This is our belvedere to which you refer?" she returned a shade stiffly. She was not sure that she should permit the feud to be disposed of by him in quite such a flippant style; even if its origins were as stupid as he depicted them.

"Of course," he said airily. "Though my father had his own more colourful descriptions of it! I expect you know that a most acrimonious exchange of letters then ensued, leading to their respective attorneys entering the lists. Our man was instructed to challenge every inch of the tower's elevation. It wouldn't fadge, of course: Sir John was entirely within his *legal* rights to build what he pleased upon his own ground," he concluded with a faint wry emphasis. Isabella then realized that he, too, was sensitive to any feeling of disloyalty in the matter of the feud, however lightly he spoke of it. Her stiffness promptly melted.

"Oh dear," she said inadequately. "No, I did not know all this, Papa never—And what happened after that?"

"Very little, I fancy—but wasn't that enough? If you had read your Greek, my girl, you would know that oceans of blood have flowed for far less reason that that. In this case, my thwarted parent took huff and sailed for his beloved Egypt and forgot all about it henceforth—except to fulminate against Blots on Landscapes, and so forth, whenever he was at home. But I think latterly it become quite a comforting ritual for him, and that in truth he would have regretted the spy tower if it had not been there."

"And to think Papa has brooded on it ever since!—idiotic man!"

"What is plain to me," Sir Ranulf mused on, "is that if Sir John had been the inheritor of our own gloomy and venerable pile, and we had lived in the plain Priory house which stood here, which my mother still hankers after, none of this damnable not-speaking would have happened! For Sir John would never then have been driven to compose all these fantasies in stone!"

"But what a monstrous silly affair all through!" cried Isabella, with a vehemence that startled him. She was reflecting that she could have known Sir Ranulf for years, instead of weeks, had it not been for her father's eccentricities. "Forgive me—it is just that I find it hard to excuse Papa for making us strangers for so long," she murmured awkwardly.

Despite the twilight, he did not miss the expression

in her eyes. He said: "Yes . . . I agree it is a cause for regret, and confoundedly ill-starred from the beginning. I find it hard to forgive too."

"Still," she said in a brighter voice, and quickening her pace a little, "we have met now: and at least that was *some* good which came out of Bianca's skitter-witted start, was it not?" She had not missed the feeling implicit in his last remark, and her spirits soared to think that he could share her sentiments in some degree. Her absolute conviction that she had at last met the man she loved, and that he, perhaps, was not altogether indifferent, enabled her to chatter away for the rest of their walk; and to fail to notice that he, for his part, was now become a shade subdued and thoughtful.

They arrived finally at the lakeside in company with the group who had been a little ahead of them on the way. At once they were surrounded by the main body of guests, who bore Sir Ranulf away upon a sea of introductions and reminiscing. Isabella went off in a haze to join her mother inside the temple.

Sir John had not permitted lanterns to be hung in the trees (in case they should mar the moon's argentine light), but there were branches of candles placed upon the table in the folly, shedding a warm glow upon a magnificent display of food more in the Roman style than that of the austere earlier civilization which the little temple commemorated.

Had the table not been of thick stone it would surely have bowed under the weight of dishes heaped upon it, she thought; Mrs Woodley had excelled herself. Staithes and two blue-liveried footmen were in attendance on the guests, who were either seated on rugs by the lake or else standing about near the columns, all with plates in their hands, and engaged in the liveliest conversation.

"I daresay you never anticipated such a success as this, when I mooted a picnic party!" she said loudly in her mother's ear when they were pressed together for a moment.

"You know I did not! However, puss, I don't deceive myself—it is the Thrinbys coming which has drawn them all." Lady Malvina smiled gratefully at her daughter, adding in a lower voice: "I make no bones it is the greatest satisfaction to me to see this atrocious feud laid to rest. I *always* told your father that it was not at all the thing on *both* their parts, and the outside of enough for their poor families! *Now*, of course, he agrees—though he still will not admit it! What a handsome pair Sir Ranulf makes with Miss Rush—Rush what-is-it?"

Isabella smiled back at her excited countenance, despite the stab that she had just dealt her.

"Talking of handsome couples—" her ladyship continued indistinctly upon a mouthful of veal cake. She turned aside for a moment to recommend the same article to a passing hungry gentleman, then suffered a brief coughing fit which left her a trifle empurpled as she whispered thrillingly to Isabella: "I *do* believe our little Bianca has fixed the interest of Mr Amersham, puss!"

"You mean to say that he has *declared* himself . . .?" Upon receiving a conspiratorial nod, she said in frank amazement: "But what of Papa?—you are not saying he will give his blessing to a younger son like Mr Amersham? Even if he was the first son—Oh, the whole family make a very genteel appearance on their narrow fortune, but as for satisfying Papa?" She made an expressive face.

"That is all true, Bella," agreed her mother complacently, "but what I collect you do *not* know is that Sir John has taken Mr Amersham in the greatest liking! I saw myself how it came about: Papa was expounding—you know how he does—upon his disapproval of harming animals in the name of sport. Most of the men laughed at him, but Mr Amersham *leaped* to his defence—and with such passion and eloquence as you never heard! Now I *know* your papa, and I tell you he was quite won over to him, fortune or no fortune! I am so pleased they have met at last, aside from dealing so extremely, as I always *sensed* they would, you know! And I have had Mr Amersham in my eye for Bianca ever since we were all in Town together, he is perfect for her!"

"Mama, a tender heart and a good address will not make amends for such a lack of prospects, whatever you may say or wish for."

"Yes, but puss, the gentleman *does* have certain prospects: it seems he is desirous of taking orders, and that if he should embark upon that course there are two excellent livings which may benefice him!"

"Or may not!" Isabella said tartly. She found she could not quite rejoice at this news as her mother could. Then she exclaimed: "Mr Amersham a clergyman!" Although, when she came to consider him as such, she had to own that it was a fitting thing, somehow.

Lady Malvina was still sweeping all misgivings aside. "Papa and I have suffered much anxiety wondering what might become of Bianca should she become *èpris* with someone *wholly unsuitable*, even if eligible enough, and who might wound her peculiarly gentle nature by perhaps a single thoughtless act. But *dear* Mr Amersham is everything considerate and understanding. I have no qualms whatever in consigning her to his care—and nor, I am certain, has Papa after that so *fortunate* meeting of minds on the question of Brutal Sports." At which point the advocate at last drew a breath, beaming happily—if a shade blindly—at her daughter.

Isabella had to smile at last in the face of such eloquence. "Well, it will certainly send her into raptures, for you must know how she dotes on him."

"Indeed I know it . . . the dear child," her ladyship murmured in a failing voice, and she turned away quite abruptly to resume her duties as temple hostess.

Isabella stayed near her for a while longer and then scanned the milling throng on the grass outside—for Bianca, she told herself, but in fact she was looking for Sir Ranulf. He was nowhere to be seen now, and neither was Miss Rishworth. She sighed, and was about to help herself to a consolatory piece of her favourite turkey pie when she heard her brother's voice coming from where the one or two carriages were drawn up.

"Ah, here is Miss Isabella, ma'am," John said in tones of palpable relief. "She will be able to recommend the choicest dishes for your delectation, I am very sure!" Whereupon he favoured his sister with a rapid roll of his eyes and consigned Mrs Beckforth to her with unseemly despatch.

"Where does your preference lie, ma'am?" she said kindly. "Perhaps in the lobster patties?"

This was met with a shake of the violet-turbanned head, and a severe animadversion upon lobsters in any form.

"The goose or turkey pies are very good," she suggested next; with a touch of wistfulness, for she could see they were vanishing fast.

"Too rich by half, Miss Huggins, thank you!"

"The veal olives have been much—"

"I never trust olives: neither does Arthur," she added needlessly.

"Then may I help you to some cold meats?" Isabella tried once more, though now with very little hope.

"Oh, just a morsel of beef, then—*that* one *there*, for the other looks tainted . . ."

Isabella now abandoned all thought of turkey pie for herself; which she was persuaded would appear gross to the extreme sensibility of Sir Ranulf's sister. Instead she took up a dainty patty. "Shall I have a rug spread so that we may sit by the lake, ma'am?"

"Thank you, but I prefer to stand—if one must—in the night air."

They stepped down to the grass, Laetitia remarking upon its wetness, and Isabella noticed once the candles were left behind them that the last pale glow of day was now being ousted by the moonlight. Very soon, all the colour would be bleached from even a dress as vivid as Helen Rishworth's—which she had just recognised again around the far curve of the lake. With a heart starting to thud she tried to make out if Sir Ranulf was still with her; he was, but she discerned that others were there with them. She relaxed, bending all her attention to the no small task of entertaining Mrs Beckworth without lapsing into incivility herself.

While thus engaged for no apparent reason—and certanly not due to the influence of her present company—she was quite suddenly filled with happiness. Letting her mind drift away from Letty's endless plaints, she went back over her earlier walk with Sir Ranulf, and the way that he had spoken to her then. She had the strongest sense that not only the course of her own existence, but the lives of those around and dear to her, were now set on a good direction. All doubt had fled: she was utterly sanguine of the notion that Sir Ranulf was meant for her and she for him.

The small group along the lakeside had now wandered a little closer, and she could see the forms of Arthur Beckforth and John, next to Helen and Sir Ranulf. She said: "Shall we join your husband and our brothers over there, ma'am?" She yearned to be with her beloved again, even if they were forced to mix with others for this part of the magic night.

"There is bound to be a chill off that water, but if you wish it," came the predictably sour response. Then, as they picked their way through the steel-coloured grass, Letty made her first complimentary remark since she had joined her; and it struck into her as had none of the rudeness. "What a striking engaged couple they make—dear Miss Rishworth and my brother."

"They do, ma'am," she faltered, her throat gone dry.

"Not but what I *ever* thought his choice could meet with my approval, but really I cannot fault Miss Rishworth," Letty concluded on a note of slight wonderment.

"I had no notion . . ." she whispered brokenly.

"Why should you, indeed! I suppose I should not have divulged the matter to *you*," Laetitia said with offensive emphasis, "but it is a fact that they are to wed. I shall be obliged if you will please not spread it abroad, Miss Huggins—although we are in daily expectation of an Announcement."

"No—no, of course, you may depend on me."

Nature did not share her own sense of high tragedy; for at that very moment a furious quacking was set up by some somnolent ducks among the lake-rushes, who evidently resented this nocturnal invasion of their privacy; and a young wag in the group which had disturbed them guffawed loudly: "Let sleeping ducks lie, what!"

And so that occasion, for Isabella, was forever associated in her mind with the trivia which had accompanied it. At the time, at least the absurd diversion allowed her to regain her countenance before Laetitia, and before joining in the now totally daunting wider conversation which lay ahead of her.

In actual fact, the following talk between the six of them was of a mercifully effortless kind. Miss Rishworth was discoursing in her usual knowledgeable style, which meant that there was little call for Isabella, or indeed anybody else, to take much part. When she came up to them Helen was saying: "Mr de Hyville has been telling me he is a devotee of the Royal Institution, which is such a convenient thing, as I have wanted for an *age* to know a member—so that I might have clandestine means of spiriting books from their library!" John was cast a ravishing smile at this point. "Of course, to attend their lectures I should needs go in gentleman's guise!—which *might* be undiscovered or might on the other hand make a byword of me! What nonsensicalness that it should! I have vowed to put it to the test some day! But it will be most gratifying, for the time being, if I can wheedle their books out of someone!"

Isabella saw that Sir Ranulf wore a somewhat ineffable expression during this vivacious and startling speech. If he enjoyed the picture which his betrothed drew for him of her throwing away her reputation in that fashion, he gave little sign of it. John, however, was still gaping at Helen in reverential awe. He now declared with rash intensity: "Miss Rishworth, it will be my privilege to execute any commissions for you in London that I may! Why, it is a rare thing to find a lady who takes the smallest interest in such matters—indeed, try as I may, I seem unable to influence man, woman or child to accompany me to Town to witness the opening of the bridge at Vauxhall later this month: now, would you credit that, ma'am? Not one!"

Laetitia here saw an opening for a superior observation. "You are speaking for your own family, Mr Huggins, no doubt. But *Arthur* here has a *consuming* interest in all such scientific things."

Sir Ranulf might have been feeling bemused at the public remarks of his intended, but not to the point of missing a chance to be rid of his baneful relatives. He added his voice to the discussion. "It is certainly an occasion I should like to attend, de Hyville, but as it happens I am unable to leave home at this present. But Arthur—why don't you go up as Letty suggests? It is not every day that an iron bridge is built over the Thames."

A rare gleam of animation lit Arthur's features. "I do believe you are right, Ranulf: perhaps I should see the opening."

But if that was in fact his wish in the matter he had not chosen his words very wisely. Without a second's pause Letty swung her influence in the opposite direction. "You forget, Arthur, that we shall be able to cross it every time we drive between Town and Wimbledon. I daresay it will be the most ordinary thing in creation within a week or two, and only of interest to the *idle and profligate*!"

Arthur seemed on the whole relieved by this firm direction. "You are absolutely in the right, my dear," he said, doing his best to make amends once he had determined where his offence lay.

At that moment a footman loomed out of the dark by Letty's side to inquire if any of them wished for more food to be fetched. Some orange cheesecake was bespoken by Sir Ranulf's Choice, and Mrs Beckforth desired a very little jaune mange, to save the servant from standing about and doing nothing. By then feeling too desolated even to swallow the end of patty remaining on her own plate, Isabella handed it to the footman as he passed her.

The dreary talk of bridges had continued remorselessly, though she was too dazed to take much of it in. She did hear the unbashful Miss Rishworth addressing John again. "—so it will suit equally if we

206

travel the day after tomorrow? Capital! That will leave me ample time to inform my sister in Duke Street of my arrival."

Isabella perceived, to her faint anger and surprise, that the cause of all her distress was now intimating to her brother that she would attend the inauguration of the new London bridge with him. Listening to her more closely, she learned that she had been intending to return to the 'civilized south' in any event within the next few days; the prospect of driving with an escort 'pleased her excessively', as she said in her frank way, to John's own plain and excessive satisfaction.

In her state of mind at the time, numbed by disappointment, Isabella paid scant heed to this amiable arrangement, and shortly after that she slipped away from the group to seek welcome solitude. She saw little more of Sir Ranulf—and indeed she did not look for him—or of her brother for the remainder of the ruined night.

However, on the next day she felt that she should drop a word of warning in John's ear; even if she were not at liberty to disclose the whole tale to him of the ragmannered pair they had become tangled with. "I should not refine too much upon Miss Rishworth's letting you squire her to Town tomorrow," she said carefully. "If Sir Ranulf cannot travel with her just now, she is no doubt glad to be able to pick upon a deputy." —Which she said with less care, but with a good deal of feeling behind it.

"I'm not refining on anything," John told her huffily. "But I won't deny, Bella, that it gratifies me to make the acquaintance of *someone* who can enter into my enthusiasm, after the total lack of appreciation I meet with all the time in my own family! But you don't need to hint me—I'm not so much a slow-top to have it escape my own notice that Sir Ranulf was at her elbow for most of the picnic."

She thought that she detected a note of shared bitterness in his last sentence, but perhaps that was merely carried over from his expression of disenchantment with his family. She hoped so, in any event; it was surely enough that her own dearest hopes should be shattered by the forthcoming match.

Fourteen

John made his departure with Miss Rishworth as arranged, but startled the household by setting out at cock-crow.

Sir Ranulf, being well acquainted with the habits of the instigator of such precipitate journeys, spared a brief sympathetic thought for his neighbour when he was awakened by Helen's carriage rattling past beneath his bedchamber. He wondered how she had prevailed upon the hired postboys to arrive promptly at dawn, but soon had the answer: it was no doubt due to that same irresistible mixture of singleness of purpose, pertinacity, and indomitable spirit, which had finally established their betrothal beyond doubt and without any effort on his part.

The carriage was soon waiting impatiently at the Priory gates, and when John joined her he led the way in his dashing new curricle. After the first horse-change Helen left her maid to travel in solitary splendour in her vehicle while she sat beside John in his. At their second stop to bait she took over the ribbons from him. Even her ardent companion began to wonder then, as he stoically viewed her expert handling of the hired cattle, if it was such a good thing after all for a female to take such an uncommon interest in one's affairs.

By about the time the pair were making the third stop on their long journey, Julia and Carleton Amersham were on the point of leaving the Priory. The brother and sister were returning home by the same means of transport as they had arrived: an old-fashioned landaulet provided by Sir John. The de Hyville ladies exchanged last words with the Amershams before they stepped up. "Now, are you *perfectly sure* you will not stay with us for a little longer?" said Lady Malvina. "For since we are all to drive to Hippolita's on Monday, which is almost your direction, we could so easily travel together."

Julia gave her a grateful smile, and Isabella was glad to see that a little colour had returned to her plump cheeks after her time with them. She said: "You have been everything kind, your la'ship, and I own it is tempting to linger just two more days, but I fear we must return to Mama before she becomes *too* overset by the infantry: they will be regaining their usual bobbish spirits by now, I don't doubt!"

"You are very right, my dear. I should not cast temptation in your path so thoughtlessly. But remember now—we depend upon seeing you in Scarborough next month as we have fixed. By the by, I fancy that Sir John may ride over to Ashbeck one day while we are at Hippolita's in order to pay his respects to your father."

"Then I will come with him," Bianca softly promised her doting swain.

"No, miss, you will not," her mama said straitly.

210

"You must wait for your reunion until we all meet again at Scarborough."

There seemed nothing more to be said, and the young Amershams climbed into the carriage and were driven away.

Malvina's well-satisfied parting smile faded a little as she turned abruptly back to the house, and happened to catch the sad expression on Isabella's countenance. She reflected then that the girl had not been in her usual force the past few days; this arrangement to visit the spa was providential.

However, when the family returned from their stay with Hippolita, they found a card inviting them to Thrinby Hall before they left for the sea. After an inward struggle, Isabella's curiosity to meet Lady Thrinby and to see their neighbours' house after all these years overcame even her reluctance to suffer the emotional turmoil which, she was perfectly sure, a next encounter with Sir Ranulf must inflict on her.

The Beckforth couple had been carefully kept in ignorance of this invitation, which had been fixed by Sir Ranulf for a time when he knew they were promised elsewhere. Consequently the de Hyvilles were received at the Hall only by Lady Thrinby and her son.

He had chosen the Great Drawing-room in which to greet them, considering that it was likely to appeal to Sir John as it was their finest old Tudor apartment, and the one least encumbered with his father's foreign mementoes. In the event, Sir John scarcely noticed the latter and was unimpressed by the former; regarding his own Gothic domain as a vast improvement upon this plain original, which he found gratifyingly deficient in the romantic qualities he strove for. Presently his host bore him off to walk over the whole house, and he soon began to wonder why this really very modest ancient building should have irked him for so long.

While this tour was being conducted by the gentlemen, Lady Thrinby and Lady Malvina discovered to their happiness that they dealt well together. Lady Thrinby seemed to take more than a usual degree of interest in Isabella, or so it seemed to her mother, though perhaps that was simply an effect of her youngest daughter's keeping so mum and mouse-ish in front of the Thrinbys. (Bianca was indeed apprehensive, for she expected to come *vis-à-vis* with Gordon at any moment, and then the whole story of her take-in must be revealed at last to her elders.)

Sir Ranulf returned to them alone, having left his neighbour in the book-room examining old documents which pertained to the house. He talked generally for a little while, then disconcertingly sought leave to carry off the de Hyville girls so that they might meet 'a very young gentleman guest of mine.'

Bianca begged off from this proposal with such an indecent haste that her mama raised her brows at her, but Isabella—who throughout this visit was determined to remain dignified—rose and went to the door with him. Aside from any question of dignity, she could not but be intrigued by the prospect of finally coming face to face with the mysterious and troublesome Gordon; and she was puzzled by Sir Ranulf's mentioning him to them, as he had seemed so reserved on the subject the last time she had spoken to him of the boy.

He led her through a door she had not noticed into

212

an annexe. They did not delay there but continued on through another almost concealed door, and so came through to the Little Drawing-room. She exclaimed with surprise at the objects she saw there.

"Yes—I wondered if you might be interested," he said with a certain wryness that she could not follow.

"Well, yes, I suppose so," she murmured, her eyes darting upwards from the portable relics of ancient Egypt to the frieze of Pharaohs, gods and goddesses that had so greatly struck Miss Rishworth. "I find the whole—rather overwhelming and a shade grotesque."

"Do you now? Good!" he said with a broad smile. "Tell me—have you had word from your brother since he left for London?"

This question—seeming a complete *non sequitur*—confused her somewhat until she divined what might lie at the root of it: Sir Ranulf probably had not approved of his future wife travelling with John, and was a trifle jealous; and well he might be, she thought, recalling John's strong degree of interest in that popular quarter. In measured tones she answered: "No, I fear that John is the world's worst correspondent. I daresay the next we shall hear from him is when he takes it into his head to return home again."

"Ah," said Sir Ranulf enigmatically. "Pray be seated, if you wish, ma'am."

She glanced at the odd-shaped antique seat he indicated, then looked back at him in some puzzlement. "You intend to summon the boy *here*? Forgive me, but is that wise, with so many rare things he might damage as boys do?"

"Good Lord no! Gordon never sets foot in here—or I fervently hope not! I must explain," he continued hastily, observing the baffled expression settling more deeply over her countenance. "Indeed I do wish you to meet Gordon, but first I wanted to talk to you alone. It is perhaps a little improper, and please do not feel obliged to stay in this oppressive room—only I fancied we could talk without interruption here."

"Of course," she agreed, endeavouring to sound as though it were the most commonplace situation; besides, she was resolved to stay now, however irregular and undignified it might turn out.

"Thank you, Miss de Hyville. What I have to say will not take long, but perhaps you would prefer to sit?" he suggested again.

She complied, making rather a piece of work of smoothing the folds of her blue cambric dress, and waiting in rising agitation for him to speak.

He remained standing, but leaned a casual elbow on the head of a queer-looking Egyptian animal which, when she finally raised her eyes to his, made her want to giggle at quite the wrong moment.

"Miss de—Isabella, when we spoke the last time we met, we both expressed our regrets at this longstanding and idiotic feud between our families, and I, for one, was certainly sincere in that regret."

All urge to laughter fled as she gazed up at the tall figure before her, and met those gray eyes set in the attractive, strong-featured face which had haunted her ever since that first chance encounter an age ago —when they had hardly spoken except in anger over the antics of her spaniel.

"I fear I have been guilty of toad-eating your

father to a preposterous intent, but tell me candidly, now, what you consider is his opinion of me—I want no flummery, mind."

Isabella blinked in surprise, and said loudly into the stillness: "Oh, I believe you are quite first oars with Papa—he speaks of you in the warmest terms. It sounds strangely to the rest of us, I may say, to hear the name of Thrinby uttered without the most terrible imprecations!" she added, trying for a note of lightness.

But, if anything, Sir Ranulf became more serious still. He left his Egyptian support and began pacing the terracotta tiled floor. "Yes, it must do . . ." he said in an abstracted way. Then he checked by her side and looked directly down at her. In a thicker voice he continued: "You know, I thought that once I made up my mind I should meet with no further difficulty. The fact is, I feel that now I *have* known you for as long as we've been neighbours—but it is not so, and perhaps I should not speak so freely after such a short acquaintance."

Bewildered by this incoherence, she said: "Please, Sir Ranulf, don't stand upon points with me—I give my word I shan't fly into a miff and create another life-long vendetta!"

"Heaven forbid!" he cried with a brief crack of laughter. "Very well—" He was instantly serious again and she noticed his cheeks had paled. "Do you suppose that your parent is sufficiently reconciled to consider favourably a match between our two families?"

Isabella stared, changed colour herself, opened her mouth to speak and then closed it again. *What could*

he mean? He must refer to himself, and yet he was be-
trothed already!

"Yes," he said, after a further period of stricken silence, "it is my very inept way of asking you to be my
wife."

"But you can't!" she protested baldly. "What—
what of Miss Rishworth?"

He struck his forehead with his palm. "How could
you know that?—ah, Letty, of course—always the in-
fernal Letty," he muttered to himself. "Did my sister
tattle it to you directly?"

"Yes, at the picnic," she managed to say. Her heart
was thumping, her hands were clasped together to
stop them shaking, and her attention was riveted
upon him.

"It is quite true that Miss Rishworth and I entertained some thought of marrying, but it was a disas-
trous mistake. Thank God we both knew that before
it was too late."

He thought back with a shudder as to how near he
had come to facing a possible breach of promise action. His letters to Helen and her father, crying off
from the match, were already in Headcorn's hand
awaiting despatch when Lord Rishworth's own missive reached him. His lordship—clearly a most embar-
rassed nobleman—had the duty to inform him that
his daughter, after returning home from a sojourn
spent with friends in the country, now owned to
doubts over the marriage. He could not understand
the girl, he wrote with a flash of frankness amongst
his other stilted lines, but: 'Perhaps it is all for the
best.' She had left home again the very next day to
stay with her sister in London, in order, it appeared,

to share her disappointment, the baffled parent reported. He was evidently as ignorant of John de Hyville's existence as he was of his daughter's prolonged stay at Thrinby Hall. And thus had Sir Ranulf been able to extricate himself from his entanglement with the Rishworths with an ease which he had never dared to envisage.

"I am sorry," he continued to Isabella, who was still struck dumb by his last words, "but I had not the faintest notion that the affair was known beyond this house. Now, I suppose, you must not only judge me as one who is prone to making rash proposals, but also conclude I am despicably *volage*—but it is *not so*, I give you my word! Lord, as I am making such a mull of the business, surely it can be believed that this is my first attempt at actually asking someone to marry me!" he said dryly. Then, with total seriousness: "Isabella—I know, with a conviction that is quite unshakeable, that you are the one I love. Your picnic party truly did prove sublime for me, for it was there I realized that I loved you."

It was impossible to doubt his sincerity, and Isabella had not the smallest desire to do so; but she was still stunned and bereft of the right words. "I am sure you will understand, sir," she murmured at last, "if I do not straightway give you my answer . . ." As she mouthed these words she stared unseeingly ahead, but then she caught his eyes and intercepted a gaze of such anxious and loving intensity that she thought: *I must be all about in my head to be talking such fustian!* "Oh, yes!—there is nothing I should like more than to be your wife!" she blurted out in a quite different strain.

"You mean it?" he asked softly. "You have not given the matter the profound consideration you first intended, I fear!"

"I didn't need to," she told him simply.

His face broke into a broad smile as he held out his hands and drew her upright. They stood face to face for a moment, then he said: "It's strange, isn't it, how sure one feels about the right person?"

She nodded, and answered him with her eyes; again her speech was gone, this time from sheer happiness. He raised her hands and kissed them, not taking his adoring gaze off her for a second. At last he said reluctantly: "Come, I think perhaps the moment has now come for you to meet Gordon—after this brief distraction!"

But she was only half-listening to this talk of Gordon, mixing it dreamily with her own thoughts. "Only think—if Bianca had been wishful to see him again, then—then we couldn't have had our *tête-à-tête* here," she murmured, aghast at that possibility.

"Oh, I felt sure a mention of Gordon's dreaded name would keep her rooted to the spot!" he told her with a certain complacency, leading her towards the main door of the Litte Drawing-room, which he unlocked with a key from his pocket.

"Am I to understand you always lock in the ladies you propose to?" she said with a sudden nervous gaiety.

He assumed a look of deep hurt, but with a belying gleam in his eye. "Didn't I tell you it was the first time I have attempted such a thing?—it seemed a wise precaution to leave you no escape!" He relocked the door behind them, adding more seriously: "No, it is just to keep Gordon at bay from father's treasures. Now, my dearest, as we make our way to the stables, where I collect the young gentleman is to be found, I should like to tell you his rather singular story. No one else knows it—not even my mother—and no one must. However, there are obvious reasons for enlightening *you*, now that you are to become—"

He fell silent as they came to the head of the broad staircase and Headcorn was seen crossing the hall below. Going down to him, Isabella smilingly declined the offer of her pelisse from the blank-faced butler and stepped outside with Sir Ranulf. The latter chuckled, observing: "That fellow is awake upon every suit, like all his kind. The news will now be all around the Room before I have even addressed your father!" He took her arm cosily within his, turned their steps towards the stable buildings, and continued with what he had begun telling her in the house.

"His mother was a young woman who lived very respectably, I believe, after Gordon's birth: though I cannot vouch for her conduct before that event. As to the man she was convinced was the father, he will certainly be known to you. The boy's name itself is something of a hint, for the mother called her child after him—George Gordon Byron."

"Lord Byron!" she ejaculated, round-eyed: this was something that even Bianca, in her wildest romantic imaginings, had not dreamed of!

"I beg you will keep your voice low," Sir Ranulf told her almost sternly, then he went on in an undertone himself: "I don't know how well acquainted you are with his lordship's somewhat colourful life, but he married last year, obtained a Deed of Separation

219

from his wife in April of this year, and promptly quit England—he maintains for ever."

"Yes, of course: his conduct was the chief *on dit* in Town at the beginning of the season, I remember."

"How extraordinary to think you were in London just when I was!" he exclaimed, greatly struck by this coincidence and for the moment diverted, lover-like, from the truly extraordinary events he was relating to her. "Yes, well—it was hardly to be expected that Gordon's mother would not make it her business to follow his lordship's movements with the keenest interest, and I regret to tell you that shortly after he left this country she—drowned herself."

"How dreadful . . . But was it really attributable to that circumstance? What I mean to say is that I could the more follow her actions if she had taken such a drastic step seven years before."

"Possibly: but, you see, throughout that time she claimed to have secured a degree of support from him in the way of money. Once he took final flight for the Continent, then she may well have despaired of any further help from that quarter. As I said, she had lived respectably but in straitened circumstances. What means she had, and from whatever source, appeared to go unstintingly on Gordon's welfare. She died almost penniless."

"I see . . ." Although in fact she saw very little as yet. "Were there any letters or evidence of some sort?"

"I cannot say as to letters, but of evidence I'm sure there is none. In spite of never having a feather to fly with himself, Lord Byron is not an ungenerous man, and the money may have signified nothing more than concern for her plight. It would seem foolish of him beyond anything—but I stress that I have not been made privy to all the details of the case. I was approached solely as a known old acquaintance of his lordship—but not *too* well-known—and asked to take temporary and secret custody of the boy until it became clear whether he would be acknowledged or not. It has all taken time, of course, because of letters having to be sent abroad, but I have heard now that the boy is completely disowned: with a somewhat dispassionate recommendation from the legal go-between that he should be thrown on the parish."

"Oh, but you cannot do that!" Isabella cried at once.

Sir Ranulf smiled the rather sweet smile that she still hardly recognized. "Take care what you say! For what I decide in this matter is likely to have a profound effect upon you now, is it not?"

She blushed and smiled back at him, only gradually remembering to say: "It does not alter the case. Such a child must not be condemned to a life of squalid misery."

"I should defer your judgement until you are more familiar with the young rascal, if I were you! He displays a considerable talent for making my life a misery sometimes, may I remind you! Don't forget either that his parentage is most dubious, whether or not he has inherited the Wild Byron Blood—as your suggestible sister might put it!"

"But you are—that is, you *were* acquainted with his lordship. Do *you* think that he—?"

"Remember, I never saw the mother: but yes, the lad has the colouring and the looks, in my view. But it is a mere possibility, no more than that, and I very

221

much doubt it could ever be proven. Byron has no sons to my knowledge, only a legitimate daughter. It surprises me that he should not recognize Gordon, as it could have been accomplished under the rose, *if* he in fact did believe Gordon was his own. However, I believe his affairs are in a worse turmoil than usual at present, and if he has no intention of ever coming back to England—" He shrugged emphatically.

"You were fearful that someone—Bianca!—might have kidnapped Gordon, were you not?"

His fond returning glance grew a trifle shamefaced. "That was a little over-fanciful, I admit. But at the time I was prey to all manner of alarms that Gordon's supposed illustrious connexions might be more widely known than was thought, and that Lady Byron, perhaps, might hear a whisper and try to take charge of him to spite her husband: it would not have been wonderful if she had attempted some-such start, you know, and her family home is in the north and lies not very distant from here."

The stable clock-tower could be seen by them now, and there came an unmistakable "Yee-ee-ee-ee!" from that direction which made Sir Ranulf emit a deep groan. Isabella laughed. "Doesn't he frighten your horses?"

"Apparently not, they seem to find it soothing!"

Isabella soon found that the handsome little boy both respected and doted upon her future husband. Whether those auburn-tinted curls and dark, irresistible eyes were Byronic or not, it seemed they would never know for certain; but whatever else fate might have in store for Gordon, she resolved there and then that he should never see the inside of the poor-house.

When she and Sir Ranulf were walking back to the house she said: "I think he will make an enchanting—" She hesitated, then added softly: "—eldest son."

"And let us hope Sir John may say much the same of me in a moment's time!"

Let COVENTRY Give You
A Little Old-Fashioned Romance